I0524796

SYLVIA MERCEDES

THE VENATRIX CHRONICLES BOOK 7

© 2020 by Sylvia Mercedes

Published by FireWyrm Books

www.SylviaMercedesBooks.com

All rights reserved. No part of this publication may be reproduced, stored in a retrieval system, or transmitted in any form or by any means—for example, electronic, photocopy, recording—without the prior written permission of the publisher. The only exception is brief quotations in printed reviews.

This volume contains a work of fiction. Names, characters, incidents, and dialogues are products of the author's imagination and are not to be construed as real. Any resemblance to actual events or persons, living or dead, is entirely coincidental.
Cover design by Deranged Doctor Design

This one is for you, Handsome, for believing in me when I don't have the strength to believe in myself. You are my true love, my hero. And you have great hair.

THE VENATRIX

Drauval Borough

Skada Mountains

Aalis River

Castra Brocar

Wodechran

Sang River

Iehanor City

CHRONICLES

Aldreda Borough

The Great Barrier

Dulimurian

The Witchwood

Sang River

KINGDOM
OF
PERRINION

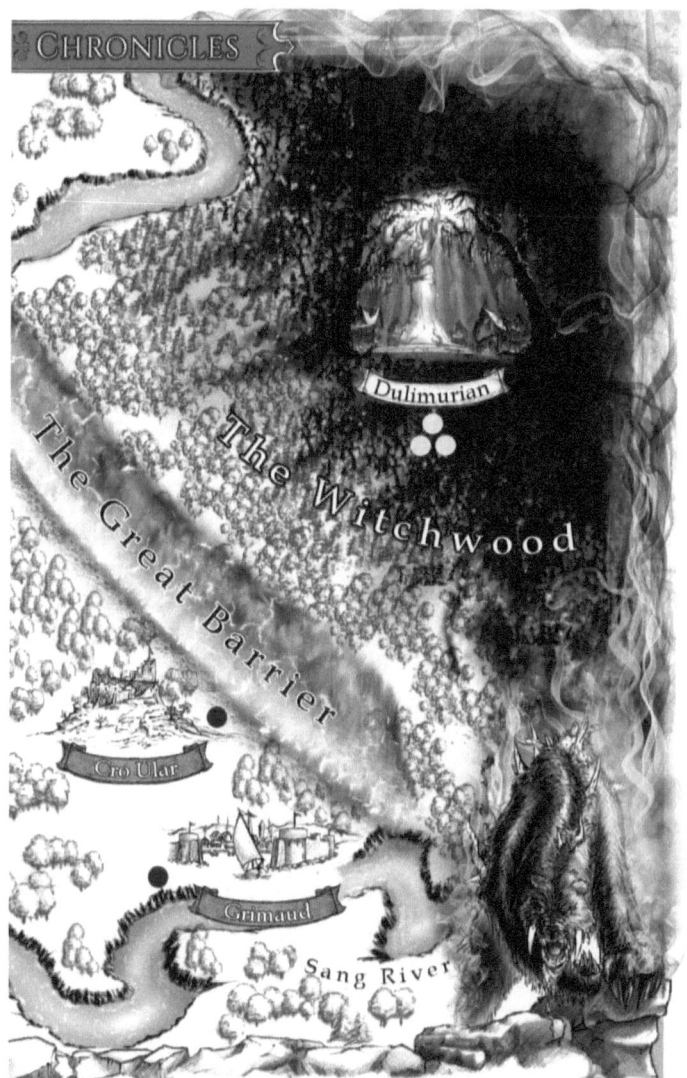

Dulimurian

The Witchwood

The Great Barrier

Cro Ular

Grimaud

Sang River

GLOSSARY OF SHADES

Shades: Disembodied spirit-beings who have escaped from their hellish dimension—the Haunts—and entered the mortal world. They cannot exist in a physical reality without mortal hosts, whom they possess and endow with unnatural powers. If left unchecked, they will gain ascendancy within a host-body and oust the original soul, taking full possession.

The following are the known varieties of shades as catalogued by the Order of Saint Evander:

ANATHEMAS
Abilities pertain to blood and curse-casting.

APPARITIONS
Abilities pertain to mind control and manipulation.

ARCANES
Mysterious entities with abilities not fully understood, but which seem to pertain to energies such as heat, motion, light, magnetism, and electricity.

ELEMENTALS
Abilities pertain to the natural elements of wind, fire, water, earth.

EVANESCERS
Abilities pertain to *evanescing*, or instantaneous distance-travel.

FERALS
Abilities pertain to heightened senses, augmented strength and agility.

LURES
Abilities pertain to enchanting voices and siren calls.

SEERS
Abilities pertain to visions, foretelling, and predictions. May also look into the past.

SHIFTERS
Abilities pertain to temporary transformation of host-bodies.

TRANSMUTERS
Abilities pertain to the transformation and manipulation of material substances.

PROLOGUE

CERINE STOOD ON THE BATTLEMENTS OF THE HIGHEST tower of Dunloch Castle. Winter winds whipped through the thin fabric of her gown, knifing her skin, for she had forgotten to wear a cloak when she limped up the tower stairs and assumed this solitary watch from above. Yet she barely felt the cold.

Her gaze was fixed on the Witchwood, a dark stain on the eastern horizon.

She'd taken up this position several hours ago now,

while the sun was yet high. It was beginning to set behind her now. Soon night would cover the land. But the darkness hovering on the far horizon had nothing to do with nightfall. It had spread throughout the day, even when the sun was at its highest point in the heavens. It poured out across the countryside of Wodechran Borough, a slow creep at first, now a flood. Through that darkness, Cerine watched a gleam of blue like a lighthouse lantern cutting through the storm, warning of disaster ahead. Yet somehow her soul felt drawn toward that glow rather than repelled by it. Perhaps disaster was her destiny.

The destiny of all Perrinion.

She started suddenly at a cold touch on her hand and looked down into the sweet round face of Nilly du Bucheron. The child had crept up the tower stairs on silent feet and now slipped her little fingers into Cerine's, gripping tight. A strange light gleamed in the child's eyes, the only physical sign of the inborn spirit dwelling inside her.

Cerine's throat tightened, but she squeezed Nilly's hand gently. "Tell me," she said, "can you see the end?

Can you see what this night will bring?"

She didn't ask the question she longed to put to the little Seer, the question that burned on her tongue, burned in her heart. To speak it aloud would be to give way to her fear, which she could not do. Not now. Not while she still drew breath.

Nilly turned away from Cerine, gazing out across the frozen Holy Lake, across the forests and fields of Wodechran Borough, but seeing far beyond. No doubt her shadow sight carried much farther than the limits of Cerine's mortal vision. But she said nothing. She offered no prophecy, bestowed no vision.

Instead, she leaned into Cerine's side and buried her little face into the folds of her skirt.

Cerine choked back the sob welling in her throat and wrapped the girl close, grateful in that moment for this small, trembling body. Nilly might possess powers beyond mortal imagining. But just now she needed Cerine's strength. And Cerine could be strong for others if she had to be. Even when she couldn't be strong for herself.

Her left hand tightened into a fist, crushing the

parchment she held. The unopened letter. Gerard's letter. Her lips moved, forming the words of a prayer song, whispering them into the winter wind.

"GoddessHead have mercy. GoddessHeart have mercy. GoddessSoul have mercy."

The sun set. Shadow fell across the land, relieved by neither stars nor moon nor heavenly bodies. Only that distant blue glow on the eastern horizon.

CHAPTER I

AYLETH FLUNG HERSELF AGAINST THE WALL SO HARD she knocked the breath out of her lungs. Air burst from her mouth in a great gust, churning the *oblivis* in front of her face. The dark particles glinted like flying sparks.

Stones were sharp against her shoulder blades, each block cut like a large faceted gem. The alley she'd ducked into was as dark as pitch, and if she'd been limited to mortal sight, she would be completely blind.

But this wasn't a real world. The rules of reality didn't

apply here.

The edges of her body fogged, morphed, trying to disintegrate. It was only a mental image, a projection created by her mind to give herself substance in this dream. She knew none of it was real, but the knowledge didn't make her surroundings any less vivid, less convincing.

Summoning courage, she angled herself to peer from the alley, scanning the road she'd just sprinted down. *Oblivis* filmed the air, especially thick along the ground, as if it rose from the paving stones themselves. The dense fog of it obscured details of the tall buildings on either side of the road but couldn't obscure the overall sense of towering hugeness. Ayleth, who had never walked in a real city in her life, shuddered.

On impulse she reached out with her senses, searching for the soul tether linking her to her shade, grasping at that presence and those powers she was so used to having readily available. But somewhere far away in the world of matter and reality, her body lay unconscious, hands bound in iron shackles. The influence of iron penetrating her skin, blood, and spirit drove her shade into deep suppression. Laranta couldn't reach her, not in that world and not in this dream. The soul tether connecting them remained intact, but it was drawn so thin that Ayleth could scarcely detect it at all.

She was alone.

The *oblivis* drifting lazily on soft currents and eddies of air suddenly seemed to shimmer and vibrate, charged with an energy that increased by the moment. Ayleth's breath caught, and a stone fist squeezed her pounding heart. She needed to pull back into the alley, to hide, but somehow couldn't tear her gaze away.

A shadow approached down the center of the road, a figure without clear form or feature. The *oblivis* in the air around it flared brighter with shadow-light, creating a pulsing aura and outline. As it approached, the negative space at its center seemed to solidify, becoming the recognizable silhouette of a tall, thin woman. No eyes gleamed in that space where a head should be. Nevertheless, Ayleth felt a gaze searching for her.

At the last possible moment she pulled back behind the wall, too frozen with terror to move. It was a hopeless game of cat and mouse. This entire world—the images of the tall buildings, the paving stones beneath her feet, even the alley in which she hid—all of it was illusion. Only the *oblivis* was real, truly real.

Ayleth ground her teeth and peered down the length of the alley. The space between the two tall buildings was narrow, thickly clogged with *oblivis* . . . and a dead end. Haunts-damned idiot that she was, letting fear drive her into hiding when she should have put as much distance between herself and her pursuer as possible! Too late. Now she'd gone and trapped herself like a—

No. She blinked, shook her head, and looked again. No, there was a door at the end of the alley after all.

With a gasp of relief on her lips, Ayleth peeled herself off the wall and half ran, half staggered to the end of the alley. The door was low, made of some material she didn't recognize. It stood open a crack. Nothing but darkness was visible beyond. She put out an eager hand . . . but hesitated. It was too easy—too convenient an escape arriving at too convenient a moment. How could she know this wasn't another trap? She didn't control this dream.

Cursing bitterly, she studied the walls on either side.

As though by magic, their faceted stones had smoothed into sheets of glass-like hardness. Nowhere to stick a finger or a toe. She couldn't climb. And she couldn't go back.

Ayleth glanced back over her shoulder, down the length of the alley, which, to her *oblivis*-dazzled vision, seemed to simultaneously both stretch and compress. At any moment, that shadowy half-formed image would appear at the alley's mouth, and its burning eyes would fix upon her with terrifying intensity. She must act. She had to escape.

Ayleth pushed the door open wider and ducked inside. She stood at the base of a narrow staircase and, having no other options available, pulled the door shut behind her and began to climb. Her bare feet made no sound on the cold treads as she took two, then three steps at a time. At first, the way led straight up. Then it began to spiral, turning round and round on itself in ever-tightening turns. The treads were almost too narrow for her feet, and Ayleth had to reach forward, using her hands to climb.

Suddenly, light. Blue, pulsing light gleamed on the wall

above her from a source out of sight around the next spiral.

"*Haunts!*" she breathed, and stopped. She couldn't go this way. She couldn't! She knew exactly where it led.

She glanced to either side. The stairwell was narrow and windowless. No landings, no doors. She turned to look back but saw only *oblivis*. She couldn't even make herself believe that the stairs she'd just climbed still existed below her.

The air began to hum with renewed energy. She felt footsteps vibrate through the stones, approaching from below. Drawing nearer with every turn.

"*Laranta!*" The silent scream burst from her soul, stretching along the soul tether. But her shade did not, *could not* answer.

Casting a hopeless gaze upward, Ayleth started, scarcely believing what she saw. A landing appeared like a miracle where there had been only wall moments ago. A gaping space of at least eight feet lay between her and the edge of that landing, with a chasm of impenetrable darkness below. She didn't hesitate. Her muscles bunched like a cat's, and she leaped, arms pinwheeling as she hurtled through the air. Her stomach struck the edge of the landing, her arms outstretched, her feet kicking over the void.

She managed to get one knee up and hoisted herself into a safe position. Crawling across the narrow space to a door set deep into the wall, she grabbed the latch. It gave at her touch, swinging open so fast that she fell through. Pushing upright, Ayleth began to scramble to her feet but froze in a crouch.

Her face went slack with shock.

She was in a dark, domed chamber. She couldn't see the apex of the dome, so high did it arch into the dense shadows overhead. Directly beneath its unseen center stood a chair—a large chair of old, treated wood, stained with splatters of blood and other substances without name. Ayleth blinked, and some of the formless void on the edge of the room coalesced into featureless hooded figures. Only one of their number formed with perfect clarity so that Ayleth could see her face.

She was a young woman—Ayleth's own age perhaps, or a little younger. Her hair was long and fell in dark waves down the back of her white linen undershirt. She wore the quilted trousers of a venatrix, but unwrapped and loose around her calves, and her bare feet padded across the cold stone floor. Two of the featureless forms led her to the huge chair, and she sat in it willingly. Stout leather straps secured the girl's legs to the chair, and Ayleth smelled the unmistakable stink of iron in the fastenings. Another strap went around her neck, and another around her forehead, securing her head to the tall back of the chair. Only her arms were left free. She clutched a set of bone Vocos pipes in her lap, her knuckles white with tension. Her wide eyes glimmered with unspoken fear, but she carefully schooled her features into a mask of courage.

The expression looked . . . no, *felt* familiar. Ayleth herself had worn it too many times.

The shadowy figures stepped back. Movement in the gallery above drew Ayleth's attention. More shadows emerged, ringing the lower part of the dome. They stood with their right arms upraised, their scorpioni aimed at the girl in the chair. Ayleth could almost taste the bitterness of Gentle Death in the air.

"Odile di Mauvalis"—the solemn voice came from

the foremost of the shadowy figures standing before the chair—"the time has come. Everything rests on you."

"I . . ." Panic laced that one word, but the young woman swallowed hard, blinked, and firmed her jaw. "I am ready to serve the Saint, according to the will of the Goddess."

Sensing more movement at the corner of her vision, Ayleth turned to see two more shadowy forms approach, carrying a cage between them. Within that cage was a rabbit. But not a tame, docile little rabbit. This creature flailed and kicked and tore at the cage wires, bloodying itself in its thrashings. Shade-taken, Ayleth realized.

The foremost of the shadowy figures now approached the cage and drew a knife. "Odile di Mauvalis," it said, "having taken the sacred vows before the altar of our Goddess, you are now called upon to accept into your mortal frame this infernal power. From this day forth, the purity of your soul and body are compromised, and unless intervention is made, you face damnation. This fate you accept according to the sacrificial precedent set by our holy forefather, Evander of Roihm. May the Goddess never turn Her gaze from you in your wretched state; may

She see the acts you will perform in Her name and count them to your credit when the day of Final Judgment comes. May She stretch out Her hand to protect you, who have dedicated your life to Her service and the protection of Her creation."

"So let it be," intoned myriad voices from the shadows beyond the torchlight.

The girl in the chair did not speak. All her vows had been said; all her words were used up. The expression on her face seemed to mirror Ayleth's own as she watched that shadowy figure fling open the top of the cage and grasp the rabbit by the back of its neck.

It all happened so fast. One moment, the rabbit screamed, high, piercing, and utterly vicious. Then, a flash of steel, a spurt of shade-blighted blood.

The domed chamber exploded with the magic of a loose, untethered shade. A shade of power beyond anything Ayleth had ever before encountered. It screamed free from its mortal-host prison, the sound of its voice tearing through Ayleth's spirit like a chorus of knives. She clapped her hands to her ears, but it was no use. The shade careened wildly up and around the dome, an invisible storm of magic and malice. The figures standing in the gallery staggered but braced themselves and did not shift their aim away from the girl strapped in the chair.

Ayleth felt the shade strike against multiple wards and barriers erected to keep it imprisoned in that chamber. She felt those spell songs quake on impact, yet they held. The shade was trapped. It must take a host body soon, for if it did not . . . Already the air shimmered as the Haunts opened to reclaim its lost spirit. Reality cracked.

Sensing its impending doom, the shade ceased its wild shrieking and seemed to assess the souls in the chamber, the incarnate bodies it needed in order to survive. Only one among all that crowd was untaken. Untaken and bound to the chair like a lamb to the altar.

The Haunts yawned. The shade made its choice. Gathering itself in dark coils, it streaked toward those wide dark eyes. Odile di Mauvalis screamed with pain. A scream that Ayleth echoed.

But through the screaming, Ayleth heard another voice deep inside her whisper eagerly, urgently: *Was I afraid when they told me my time had come? Of course not. I was special. I would survive my Possession, and I would master the Elemental shade they gave me. I would master the* oblivis.

Ayleth turned. Who was that standing in the darkness beside her? One of the many shadow figures of this vision, formless phantoms of a long-ago memory? Or was it . . .

She didn't wait to find out. She broke into a run, dashing through the images around her. They disintegrated like vapors, and the dome vanished. The sounds, the spells, the screams faded to nothing. For ten pounding footfalls she ran in utter darkness.

Then she was out on a broad road under a heavy, dark sky. The towering structures of Dulimurian loomed around her, gaping windows like hundreds of watchful eyes through which only one dark soul watched. She pushed on through the fog of *oblivis,* running faster, running until she could no longer hear that voice in her head, could no longer hear the echoes of the Possession in her ears.

Why was this happening to her? Why did that insistent voice pursue her so relentlessly, whispering these stories and planting these memory images in her head? It was as though—Ayleth grimaced, hardly daring to admit the thought—it seemed as though Odile might be trying to make her *understand*. By forcing her to see those moments, to live them.

But that could not be. It must be a trap of some kind. Because Odile should want nothing more than to kill Ayleth, who was the last stumbling block between the Witch Queen and the immortality offered by the *Cravan Druch*.

Ayleth growled as she ran on up that broad road, which led across a bridge to another tangle of smaller streets where she might temporarily hide. She would not be manipulated; she would not be lulled. She would not let her guard down, not for a moment.

And she would not let herself care about the dark-eyed girl strapped to the chair. That girl who was so familiar, so . . .

Ayleth staggered to a halt just as she reached the far side of the bridge, panting hard. "Haunts *damn!*" she cursed. The landscape had shifted before her again. The lower city she had sought in hope of shelter vanished, giving place to a massive monolith tiered with stairs carved directly into the stone. And, standing atop that monolith in an attitude of victory and power, the mighty idol of Odile, her hand outstretched above her city.

A blue light glowed high above, resting in the palm of that hand—a glow of *eitr* and, pulsing beneath it, an aura of power.

Ayleth growled in frustration and took a sharp turn. A wall rose before her, but it wasn't tall. She leaped, scrambled to the top, and paused a moment to catch her breath, peering down into the gloom on the far side. A twelve-foot drop to stone paving.

Grimacing, she lowered herself over the edge, suspending her body from her fingertips, then dropped and rolled down a rocky incline, her hands scrabbling at stone and shrubs, her eyes blinking in the sudden light of day. At its base, she flipped over and lay still a moment while rain pounded her face, soaking her to the skin. She lay on a narrow track leading up the side of a mountain surrounded by other rocky peaks.

Sounds of battle filled the air. Red Hoods flashed in her vision; shouts rang out in the crisp mountain air. And magic. Magic reverberated against the stone crags and cliffs, deadly and varied, all the different spirit colors of shades flashing before her vision.

Ayleth pulled herself upright on that narrow track, her feet slipping in the mud. Through the chaos, she saw a horse rear, staggering, and saw the rider spring free as the beast fell. Ayleth swept rain from her eyes and saw a familiar face looking out from behind the horse's collapsed form—that same dark-eyed young woman from the domed chamber. Older now. Harder. Fiercer. And full of some secret anger that simmered in her soul.

As Ayleth watched, she saw the woman pull a set of Vocos pipes from their sheath, put them to her lips, and begin to play the Song of Summoning. Power roiled in her spirit; dark magic rose from her core. Strands of suppression songs still held it in place, however, and the young woman worked frantically to disentangle them.

A figure rose in the air before her—a man riding on wind currents, surrounded by the ascendant magic of his Elemental shade. Ayleth watched through the curtain of rain as he fixed his gaze on the young venatrix, stretched out his hand, and twisted his wrist. An arm of air reached out, wrapped around the woman, and hurled her into the open air. She plunged down into the wooded valley below and out of sight.

I did not wake. For days, for weeks even, I lay in a stupor, trapped inside my own mind, the voice whispered in Ayleth's ear.

The images changed. The mountain vanished. The rain melted away. More scenes presented themselves before her vision, one after another. And this time, Ayleth didn't run. She didn't even try. She could not tear her gaze away from the incredible history playing out before her. The story of this young woman who was so like Ayleth herself. Brought up to believe in her singular and vital purpose. Devoted to the Goddess and the Law of Saint Evander. Loyal, strong, ambitious, determined . . . yet never deemed good enough.

That subtle voice murmured in Ayleth's ear, but Ayleth was hardly aware of it now. She saw, heard, smelled, and tasted each scene as though she had stood there, silent and unobserved in the shadows all along.

She saw the ferocious young venatrix snarl at the man trying to heal her.

She saw the same venatrix resting in the arms of that man as the two of them gazed into the face of their daughter.

Olena.

She saw the Red Hoods return to the mountains, creeping through the forest and up the slopes.

She saw the young venatrix crawl out from a tent, her limbs still half paralyzed with poison as she gazed up at a stream of smoke rising in the sky. And she watched that same young woman, sick and thin and pale, her eyes hollow in a skeletal face, climb up through the mountain, searching, searching, searching until she found the remains of a pyre.

A stab of agony shot through Ayleth's soul, and tears streamed down her face. She wept along with the venatrix. She wept with Odile as she sank to her knees in the middle of those cold ashes, burying her hands, burying her face, screaming, choking, heaving.

"*Olena,*" Ayleth whispered.

Then she gasped, dismayed. What was she doing? Standing here like a fool, not even trying to resist that voice in her head.

Ayleth wrenched away from the scene and ran into the whirling *oblivis*. Fear chased at her heels, fear of the change she felt in her heart. She knew the truth. She *knew* it, Goddess help her! Odile was a monster, a witch, an abomination in the eyes of divinity and goodness. She had unleashed the evil of shade-taken magic on Perrinion, destroyed temples, and razed holy sites. She slaughtered mortals and drove them before her like slaves. To feel sympathy, to feel empathy for such a fiend could only mean . . .

"*No!*" Ayleth snarled and drove her spirit faster in flight. The *oblivis* parted before her, accepting her into its depths, filling her senses so that she could no longer hear the venatrix's weeping behind her.

But that voice pursued her, relentless as death: *Wait, child. Do not run from me.*

Ayleth dared not stop, dared not listen. She was poised on the edge of the precipice, and if she stopped to listen to that voice, she knew she would fall forever. So she surged forward, allowing her spirit to turn in a certain direction—a direction toward which she had been pulled like a compass arrow pulls north, but which she had tried to fight all this while.

She turned to the idol. To the *eitr* crown waiting

above.

The city manifested around her once more, clear and crisp—not a ruin, but rather the memory of the city as it once had been, bright and shining beneath the sun, every black surface refracting many-colored prisms of color. The image of the idol towered over all. Not Odile's idol. No, the beautiful, carved face looming overhead was similar to that of the Witch Queen but not the same.

Ayleth ducked her head, refusing to look, and redoubled her pace. She feared that idol, feared that Presence waiting for her up above. But just then she feared her pursuer more. She leaped up the endless black steps ascending the huge monolith of pure oblidite that supported the idol, then raced across the top of the monolith to the idol's right foot, where she found a door set into the ankle in such a way that it was almost invisible. She reached out her hand, but the door opened before she could touch it.

A stair spiraled up before her eyes. Ayleth bounded forward, taking three treads at a time. Feeling reality warp around her, she knew that the power waiting for her at the top of the stair was condensing her journey, enabling her to climb much faster than she could in the physical world. She arrived at a door that, when she opened it, led to a bridge stretched out across an open expanse of air nearly a mile above the world below. Ayleth choked on her own breath, dizzy and sick; but through the haze she recognized the bridge as the idol's right arm. At the end of it waited the outstretched palm. And the crown.

Ayleth's determination failed her. The blue light cupped in that distant hand pulsed urgently, bidding her to hasten, but she couldn't make her feet obey, couldn't force them to step out onto that bridge.

Then the air around her ears vibrated again with power, and she heard Odile's voice whisper: *There is much more you must know, much more I must tell you.*

With a thin sob sticking in her throat, Ayleth hurtled forward, away from the shelter of the staircase and out into that open air. Wind blew in her face, *oblivis* stinging her skin and eyes like grains of sand. She caught glimpses of the city below, the concentric circles of its layout, the five-pointed star of the Queen's Highways all leading to this central point. But she dared not look long or her courage would surely shrivel to nothing. Above and behind her, she felt the enormous face of the idol looking down, its empty eyes mildly curious. But she refused to look back, to see those features—her own features— magnified to such a terrible degree. She raced full speed along the length of the arm and leaped at last into the space between the pillars of the four fingers and thumb.

The crown waited in the center of the palm. It was bigger than she'd anticipated. Much bigger. She'd glimpsed it only once before, months ago, in another dream. Then it had encircled Odile's head, and though it was huge, towering a full foot high, it had not been too large for the queen's skull.

This crown, however . . . It could easily fit a giant twice Odile's size. Its tines were fashioned with cruel elegance, graceful as the unfurled leaves of a lily, but sharp as blades. The strange *eitr* of which it had been formed glowed with inner life. Holy writ said *eitr* was the substance from which the Goddess created all living matter. The blast of the crucible, the torture of hammer and anvil, had done nothing to alter the raging life in its core.

But like all living things, it could be possessed of a

parasite spirit.

Ayleth gazed at the crown, at the pulsing blue that seemed to flow like veins just beneath its hardened surface. She felt the Presence gazing back. She took a step toward it, one hand outstretched.

"*Stop.*"

CHAPTER 2

FROM THE CORNER OF HER EYE, HOLLIS COULD JUST see the venator and venatrix searching the bodies of the dead shade-taken littering the highway, searching for poison darts to refill their quivers. She didn't know their names. She had rarely visited Castra Breçar over the last twenty years, and the young faces of her brethren were unfamiliar to her. The venator looked near thirty years old and boasted a light-colored beard now stained with shade-blighted blood. The venatrix was younger still, hardly older than Ayleth.

Hollis heard the venatrix gasp when she rolled over the body of one of the dead monsters. Hollis couldn't see what the girl saw, which was probably just as well, for the venatrix turned and heaved, her body jolting with horror. No one moved to comfort her, to offer her aid. She was a venatrix. And when the spasms finally passed, she set to work, pulling darts from the creature's hide, studying them to see if any poison remained on their tips.

Hollis bowed her head. She knelt on the polished black oblidite pavers of the Queen's Road, surrounded by carnage. Beyond the road loomed the Witchwood. The poisonous Witchwood, whose mind she'd penetrated and whose wrath she'd stirred. It was quiet for now . . . deathly quiet. It would be easy to believe that it slept, but Hollis knew better. It didn't sleep. It merely waited.

Her hand felt along her various quivers, counting poisoned darts. Only three Gentle Deaths remained to her. A few other poisons as well, less useful, though she was glad to have them. Beyond that, she had her knife, her iron spike, and, of course, her shade. It would have to be enough.

She lifted her head, peering over the long point of her beak mask to where Fendrel stood a few paces away. His body was upright, his stance wide, his face turned away from Hollis, staring into the shadows of the Witchwood. Staring into the place where Ayleth had been dragged out of view. Ayleth . . . his weapon. His last hope for redemption, snatched out from under his nose.

Hollis could hardly bear to look at him. Her shadow senses detected the devastation radiating from his soul. And it was her fault—her fault that the Witchwood took Ayleth. She had plunged recklessly into its mind, revealing Ayleth's presence, pleading with that massive other-worldly power for help. Her gamble had worked: The Witchwood had risen against the shade-taken horde of Dread Odile, slaughtering or dispersing all those twisted monsters that otherwise would surely have destroyed the small band of Evanderians.

But then the Wood had claimed its reward.

Hollis's head throbbed, still feeling as though a hundred tentacles poured into her nostrils, her eyes, her ears, and down her throat. With concentration she could shake the phantom sensation away, but if she relaxed her mind even for a moment, it all returned.

When the beat of hastening footsteps caught her ears, Hollis glanced up to see Fendrel stiffen and stare into the trees. She rose and moved to stand behind him, out of his line of sight.

A figure approached through the shadows and burst out onto the paving stones of the Queen's Highway. Venator Kephan du Tam bent in half, hands on his knees, struggling to catch his breath through his mask.

"What word, du Tam?" Fendrel demanded.

Kephan shook his head and pulled himself up sharply. "Dominus," he panted, "I followed the trail as far as possible. From what I can tell, Ayleth is still alive. I found no blood; I smelled no death; I sensed no sundered soul. But . . ."

"Speak, man!" Fendrel snarled.

Kephan grimaced, shaking his head. "I came to a wall of vines. I summoned up more of my shade's strength and tried to tear my way through. But it was impenetrable."

"And Ayleth?" Hollis asked. Fendrel shuddered at the sound of her voice behind him but did not turn.

Kephan turned his heavy gaze to Hollis. Feral light glowed in his pupils, his indwelling spirit called to high ascendancy. "Unless my shadow senses deceive me, she's on the other side."

Fendrel abruptly strode ten paces along the road they had just traveled, turning his back on the rest of them. The venator and venatrix approached Kephan, and Hollis heard him answering their questions in a low voice. She felt the tension in their spirits. All of them carried highly ascendant shades. None had bothered to strengthen the suppression spells since their recent battle. The ether was dense with spirits, human and shade. Emotions and magic shimmered together in a storm of color and sound and energy.

Hollis moved away from the other three, her eyes fixed on Fendrel's back. It was as square and strong as it had ever been. And his long hair, pulled back from his face in three tight braids, fell across his shoulders, the ends naturally curling, as soft as spun gold. The strands of gray woven through the gold were almost invisible, and from where she stood, Hollis could almost believe she gazed through time, twenty-five years ago, at the young

Fendrel. A strong, passionate soul, single-minded with purpose. How she had loved him then.

How she feared him now.

She approached him from behind, taking care to let the heels of her boots strike on the paving stones so as not to startle him. She saw by the slight turn of his head that he heard her, that he recognized the sound of her stride. She lifted one hand, wanting to rest it on his shoulder. But she stopped, her fingers hovering just inches above his leather armor, and drew a careful breath.

"She's not dead, Fendrel," she said.

He didn't answer. The muscles in his neck stiffened.

"All hope is not lost. The crown . . . it needs her. Alive. It wants her body and her blood. It would not kill her. She's alive out there. Somewhere. I know it."

"Alive, perhaps." Fendrel's voice was as deep and harsh as broken stone. "But it will take her. Use her. Possess her." He shook his head heavily, the end of his beak mask swinging like a spear. "It would have been better for us all if I'd killed her when I had the chance."

Hollis jerked her hand away as a shot of ice went through her breast. All the tender feelings threatening to cloud her judgment vanished. This man was still Venator Dominus du Glaive. Not Fendrel, not the boy she had once loved. This was the Black Hood. The legend. The liar.

She took a step back, clenching her fists at her sides, and made certain no telltale emotion tainted her voice when she spoke. "Even if the crown took possession of Ayleth, she won't be as powerful as Dread Odile once was. Without the twinned shades, she will be lesser. We could still defeat her. Defeat it." Even as the words left her mouth, she shook her head and looked off into the forest. "But she won't wear the Crown, Fendrel. No matter what it does to her. She won't."

"You're a fool if you believe that." Fendrel rounded on Hollis, his eyes burning over the edge of his mask.

"You're the fool, Fendrel. You always were." Hollis pressed a hand to her breast, feeling the thud of her heart right through her leather armor. "I know Ayleth. I raised her from childhood, and I know her soul. You have no idea who she is. You have no idea of the depths of her . . . of her stubbornness. Of her mulish, willful determination. But her heart . . ." She sighed, and the muscles of her jaw tightened. "Her heart is and always was true." Her eyes flashed. "She doesn't long for power or influence or legend. Not like you. Not like me."

Fendrel stared down at her from under his heavy brows. He studied her closely, his scrutiny like the edge of a razor going over her skin. One wrong move, and he'd cut her, draw blood in long ribbons. Hollis didn't flinch.

"There is still hope." After a pause she shrugged. "And even if there isn't, what choice do you have? Will you run back home to Dunloch? Call up some barrier spells? Or will you summon more willing souls to give their lives and eternities for the *atacara*?"

Fendrel turned away. It was impossible to read his expression through the mask, through the curtain of hair falling across his cheek. But Hollis didn't need to see his face. Her ascendant shade touched the edge of his mind.

She withdrew quickly. The pulse of his despair was too great.

Aware of her shade's touch, he looked up again. A dangerous light flickered in his eye. "What would you propose, Venatrix?" he demanded. "Have the years instilled in you an appetite for suicide?"

His words brought memories crashing back on her—memories of long ago she had all but forgotten. She saw herself as a young girl, scarcely past her Possession ceremony. Full of fire. Full of vigor. Full of fear. She saw herself standing in the armory of Castra Iarcand, her whole body shaking with emotions she hardly dared name.

"This is suicide, Fendrel!" she'd told him then. "You go to your doom."

"Better to die fulfilling the Goddess's will than to live as a coward. A worm," he had answered.

Fendrel had never doubted the Goddess's will. He never doubted the purpose he saw before him, never doubted any step he took. But where had those steps led him in the end?

"None of us know for certain what the Goddess wills for our deaths," Hollis said. "But we're not lambs to be slaughtered on altars. We are living sacrifices. We serve with our lives . . . and we let Her ordain our ends."

She straightened her shoulders and, on impulse, pulled the beaked mask away from her face so that she could look Fendrel straight on, so that he could see her clearly.

"I will march on to Dulimurian," she said. "I will do all I can to prevent Odile from reaching the crown."

Fendrel drew a long breath through his mask. Then he too slipped the straps from behind his ears and pulled the beak away, revealing his face. Hollis saw how dark his veins ran beneath his pale skin, saw how tainted his blood had become. The spirit inside him warred with his soul, and it took everything he had to keep it at bay. But he held on. Against all odds, he held on.

He took one step, then another, covering the distance between them until he loomed over Hollis, his broad shoulders blocking her view of the forest beyond him, his gaze consuming hers. How easy it once had been to lose herself in those eyes of his, to dive into those gray pools and be submerged in his will.

Not anymore. Though the air between them was alive with heat, with the power of their shades and the pulse of their hearts, Hollis would never be overcome by Fendrel again.

"Well?" she asked, her voice rasping and rough in her throat. "What will you do?"

"I will march with you, Hollis," Fendrel said. He

reached out, almost took her hand. She felt his fingers close to hers, but he did not touch her. "I will die with you."

"Then may the Goddess have mercy on our souls."

CHAPTER 3

TERRYN SIGHTED DOWN HIS ARM, HIS SCORPIONA aimed at the heart of the young woman standing across from him, not five yards away. Shadows cast by the tortured trees of the Witchwood could not fully obscure her lovely features or the soft and womanly curves of her body on prominent display through the ruins of a sumptuous ballgown.

He froze. For an instant, he saw her there—the beautiful lady who had once been the object of his youthful passion, a fantasy tantalizingly just out of reach. He couldn't separate the image before him from those memories—her seductive smile, her arms around his neck, those soft curves pressed against his body in eager invitation. The torments racking his body as he strove for the celibate control demanded by his Order.

For an instant he saw Liselle di Matin. But only for an instant.

Terryn blinked, and his shadow sight burst forcefully into his mind to reveal the ascendant shade brimming in that host body, the dangerous glow of weird Evanescer light. He set his teeth and squeezed the triggering mechanism against his palm. The scorpiona jolted his arm as it fired. The Gentle Death dart sped through the air, cutting through the motes of *oblivis* as though piercing through layer after layer of thick curtain. His eyes played tricks on him, telling him that its progress was painfully slow, though in reality he knew it sped like a flash of light.

Not fast enough. The Phantomwitch vanished in a burst of coiling darkness, stepping from this world and into the Haunts, following her invisible paths. The Gentle Death cut through the emptiness where her heart had been but a breath before. And the world ripped as she reemerged in the space just behind Terryn.

A flash of steel. Gerard's sword sliced through the air in Terryn's peripheral vision. Terryn staggered to the right, stepping away from that attack. The prince's reaction time was good, his calculation as to the place of the witch's likely reappearance nearly perfect. But his blade whistled through nothing but whirling *oblivis*, missing the Phantomwitch by a fraction. This time, she did not immediately reappear.

"Quick!" Terryn barked and grabbed Gerard by the arm. Without protest, Gerard allowed himself to be hauled several paces to one side, spun, and placed with his back against a tree so that the Phantomwitch could not step through the air right behind him. Terryn then whirled, turning his back to Gerard, placing his own body as a shield of protection. He grabbed for another Gentle Death dart from his quivers. He only had a few left.

A blazing white wing swung before his eyes. Nisirdi, his ascendant shade, stepped in front of him, long neck arched up, mouth open, burning white light brimming in its mouth. It looked this way and that, as though searching for some sign of its fellow shade spirit but unable to catch a sense of it.

Terryn paused. He wasn't used to drawing on his shade's magic in the midst of a battle, wasn't used to controlling that tremendous power. Ought he to call upon it now? Gather a blast of white light into his palm to let loose on the Phantomwitch the moment she reappeared? It might be a more effective attack than the poison, and—

The world opened in another belch of darkness, and the Phantomwitch leaped forth on Terryn's left. He turned, fired, but she was too close and too quick. She knocked his arm to one side, and the dart flew wide.

"*Nisirdi!*" Terryn roared in his head.

His shade lurched in response, and heat billowed up from Terryn's core, coursing out through his arms, to his hands. The Phantomwitch caught him by the throat, and Liselle smiled into his face.

"Come with me, Venator," she hissed.

Terryn didn't have time even to gasp.

"NO!"

The scream tore from Gerard's throat as he lunged, his hand grasping at clouds of whirling *oblivis*. He caught only emptiness where Terryn had stood. The air reverberated with the shock of worlds torn open and shut in an instant, and the sensation shook him to his bones.

Gerard staggered back several paces until he hit a tree trunk. His chest heaved. Poison coated his lungs, and weakness rippled down through his legs, pooling in his gut. He couldn't make himself believe what he'd just seen. He could only stand there, breathing hard, drawing more poison into himself.

Then he lurched into motion. At first, he could take no more than a few staggering steps. But as his resolve firmed, his strength revived, and he moved faster and faster still. He remembered what Terryn had told him, that the Phantomwitch could only move within a mile radius of a planted anchor. He didn't have much time to get outside that radius. But he could try.

He blinked—and in the darkness behind his eyelids, he saw that white hand clutch Terryn's throat. He saw Liselle's lovely face twisted with Inren's hatred. And

Fayline? What about Fayline? Was there any chance that she remained somewhere within that host? Driven insane yet somehow clinging to existence in this world?

Gerard drove these thoughts back down. He couldn't think right now. To allow any of these thoughts leeway would be to give in to despair. And if he despaired, all was lost. He had to keep moving. He must achieve the vision the Seer child had planted in his brain—that glimpse of a stone platform high above the world, the pillared fingers of a statue's hand surrounding him. Starlight gleaming on black stone . . .

He ran on. His body shook with weakness at every step he took. The poisoned air was getting to him, he knew it. The air and his own terror. His knees buckled. He fell, caught himself, pulled upright, fell again. He crawled, dragging his sword after him. The blade dug a black trench in the rotten soil.

Gerard bowed his head, muck-crusted hair hanging over his brow, plastering against his cheeks. His lungs ached with the need for fresh air, but there was none to be had for miles. His limbs tingled, and his gut churned with sickness. He crawled on, hand after hand, knee after knee. His sword was like a leaden weight, and it took all his will to drag it along.

Then he stopped.

A bare white foot filled his vision. A dainty foot, so stark, almost luminescent against the putrid soil of the Witchwood. Slowly Gerard let his gaze climb from that foot to the delicate ankle, the shapely calf, the bare knee. Upward still to ragged skirts clinging to curved thighs and a small waist.

He couldn't quite bring himself to look higher still into Liselle's face. He didn't want to see Inren gazing back at him.

"I have heard so much about you, Golden Prince," the Phantomwitch said, her words falling on his ears like drops of burning acid. "I have seen your face in my dreams more times than I can count. In *her* dreams, I should say. I feel as though we know one another quite well."

She bent and caught him by the hair on top of his head, yanking his face back so that he must meet her eyes. Gerard couldn't breathe. He couldn't think. He could only blink up at her. But, he noted distantly, almost without real thought . . . he wasn't frightened. Not really. Not anymore.

A hideous grin ripped the witch's mouth open, distorting Liselle's stolen face, displaying blood-stained teeth. She crouched and, using her free hand, snatched the sword from Gerard's unresisting fingers. With a vicious push, she set him back on his heels so that he knelt in front of her in the rot. His arms were limp at his sides, his shoulders sagging. But he held his head high even as the witch backed up several paces, even as she raised his sword.

"Your father cut off my goddess's head," Inren snarled. "I think it fitting somehow that your fate should mirror hers. Only, Odile will be queen again, while you . . ." She shook her head and chuckled cruelly. "Your head will never wear a crown before it rides high on the end of a pike."

She swung the sword back over her shoulder. It was such a strange, incongruous sight: dainty Liselle di Matin heaving that weapon. Liselle certainly didn't have the strength to cut a man's head from his shoulders with a single stroke. But she could kill him even so. She could hack and hack with that sharp blade, and it would do the trick soon enough.

Gerard swallowed hard but kept his neck straight, his gaze even. And still, he wasn't afraid. Perhaps the poison had gone to his head, had broken his sanity, his reason. It didn't matter. He looked up at the Phantomwitch. And he smiled.

She froze. The sword hovered in the air above her shoulder. Her legs were braced wide for the swinging stroke, her torso twisted. But she didn't move. Something flickered in her eyes.

Then a shuddering quake passed through her body and rippled up her spine, as though she was about to vomit. She dropped the sword, and it landed thickly behind her, nearly vanishing in mud and festering ooze. Her body shook, harder and harder, and her eyes widened. A sound rose up from inside her as though billowing up from the pit of her gut, from the crux of her soul. She threw back her head and roared to the intertwined branches overhead. The *oblivis* in the air whirled wildly as though in a gale. Gerard recoiled, lifting one hand in a futile gesture of defense.

But then the Phantomwitch bowed her head to her breast and stood before him like a stuffed doll propped on a rod, lifeless and limp, but upright. Slowly, she raised her head and peered down at him through Liselle's blue eyes.

"My love?" she said.

He knew that voice.

Gerard gasped. With an effort, he hauled himself to his feet, swaying as he stood, as unsteady on his legs as a newborn foal. She did not move, only stared at him. The echo of her voice was in his ears. He swallowed hard, tasting the foul *oblivis* on his tongue. Then he managed to whisper, "Fayline?"

A shriek ripped the air. The face before him transformed, becoming a demonic mask of rage and hunger and pain. Before he could react, she lurched at him, her curled fingers scratching like claws, catching at his shirt, his hair, his face.

The worlds broke open, and she dragged him into darkness.

CHAPTER 4

AYLETH STOOD AS THOUGH TURNED TO STONE, ONE hand still extended toward the crown. It pulsed with blue light from its core, the rhythm of that pulse increasing like a quickened heartbeat. Something, some darkness from within the confines of that tined circlet, seemed to call to her spirit, urging her to act.

But the voice of Dread Odile rang against the pillared fingers of the idol's hand. It stopped Ayleth in her tracks, and she half wondered if she was caught in a spell. She could not tear her gaze from the crown, not even if she wished to, yet somehow, with the weird perspective of dreams, she seemed to step outside of her head, to see the whole vista as though from a distance. She saw herself poised on the sloping palm of the hand in the act of stepping over its deep groove lines.

And she saw Odile standing on the arm behind her, near the delicately wrought veins of the wrist. Even as Ayleth watched, her shadowy outline took on more and more solid substance, becoming a fully projected image of a tall woman in long black robes. Her glossy hair wafted in eddies of *oblivis*—thick, lazy movements, more like water than wind.

"*Stop*," she said again, her voice soft, almost gentle. The gentleness was more compelling than if she'd screamed. "*Don't touch it, child. You don't want to—*"

Ayleth lunged.

The distant view broke, and she was once more inside her head, limited to the perspective of her eyes. She had an instant in which to decide. She knew what she'd been told about the *eitr* crown—that only those of the du Mauvalis bloodline could touch it and survive. That only

Odile herself, possessed of the twin shade, could command its powers.

It must consider Ayleth an easy conquest. It must think she would be easily tempted by the gifts it offered, that she would never once stop to consider whether the offer was real. It must expect to manipulate her into becoming its mindless host. But . . .

But this crown wasn't real. This crown was nothing but a dream. This whole world was mere figments of thought and imagination borne of the Witchwood's mind.

Ayleth's hands wrapped around the base of the crown. Though an instant before it had been far too large for her head, too huge and heavy even for her to lift without Laranta's power in her limbs, at her touch it changed, becoming just the right size, shape, and weight. She whirled on her heel so that she faced Odile just as she lifted the circlet and brought it down around her forehead.

The cold metal seemed to latch hold, pulsing into her skull, its sharp edge digging into her skin, into bone. She realized her mistake at once, but it was already too late. Power surged through her, rushing inside her head until she cried out. Her hands scrabbled, trying and failing to get a grip on the crown, to tear it free. This was not like when Laranta's strength flowed through her. This was greater, darker. Overwhelming.

Intoxicating.

The Presence was there. Trapped within the crown, lacking the channel of a mortal host through which to make itself understood by mortal minds, it was nearly incomprehensible. A being so huge, so other, so horrible, she could discern nothing but vast, twining, tangled awareness, as complex as the entire root system of the Witchwood. All there. In her mind.

For the moment . . . all *hers*.

She breathed. *Oblivis* streamed from her nostrils in black clouds.

Through those twin streams of darkness, she saw the figure of Odile descend upon her. The dark goddess, mistress of *oblivis*, reached out her hands and summoned the element to her will, shaping it into a whirling orb. Multiple rings of lethal power spun on a single axis, faster and faster, shooting off sparks of raw magic. With a flick of her wrist, Odile hurled her missile, and it streaked straight for Ayleth, straight for the crown on her head.

Ayleth responded. Her instincts were fast, too fast. So fast that she knew she didn't move of her own volition at all—some other will had taken her over. But it *felt* like her own decision, her own reaction, lightning quick and confident. She raised her hands, crossing her arms at the wrists, and the *oblivis* in the air before her face solidified into a shield. Odile's missile struck, ricocheted off, hit one of the pillar fingers of the hand, and shot off into the sky.

Odile kept coming. Another weapon already gleamed in her hands, a lance as thick around as a man's waist and sharpened to a cruel, jagged point. She sent it flying, and it tore through Ayleth's shield. Ayleth threw herself to the ground. The lance pierced the palm of the statue like a nail driven through flesh and bone.

The dream reality shivered around Ayleth, ready to disintegrate. But the power surging through her snatched for more *oblivis* and grabbed hold, forcing the dream to remain solid, forcing the perception of that stone hand to remain in place. Ayleth slid, caught her balance, and was up again in an instant. Once more the instinct that didn't belong to her pulsed. She swept one arm before her face in an aggressive arc. The air coalesced into a hundred small, ragged knives of oblidite streaking straight for Odile. The knives tore through her robes, through her flesh, and straight out the other side of her, their sharpened ends dripping with black, shade-blighted blood.

Ayleth stared at the figure before her, at the wounds riddling that tall, slender body. Wounds so small, so sharp, so swift, they had not yet begun to bleed.

Odile looked down at her shredded form, blinking demurely. Then she looked up again and met Ayleth's eye. *"You little fool,"* she said. *"Don't you realize? You have no power here. It's only a dream."*

Ayleth wasn't fast enough to defend herself this time. The attack hit before she realized it was coming. The air in front of her suddenly solidified, throwing her back. She flew so hard, she struck one of the finger pillars. She reached out, trying to catch hold of the stone, but the attack kept coming, the solid air pushing her, crushing her.

The pillar vanished.

Ayleth fell, cartwheeling through the sky, headfirst,

then feet first, then headfirst again, arms flailing, grasping at nothing. She felt the solid band of *eitr* around her forehead disintegrate, felt the power flow out from her spirit, leaving her weak, helpless, and—

She struck. The impact was so soft, she scarcely felt it. One moment she fell, the next moment, she simply lay on nothing, in nothing, as nothing. Her projected image was gone. There was only spirit, disembodied, floating in a haze of *oblivis*.

How long she remained in this state she couldn't say. Time meant nothing to her. But slowly, surely, the dreamscape solidified once more. Her mind projected a new body—she felt it taking shape, lying naked, spread-eagle, on solid ground. She felt smooth stone under her back. Heavy eyelids weighted her face, and she lifted them with an effort to find herself lying on the polished monolith beneath Odile's idol. The idol itself had crumpled to its knees, left arm broken clean away, head severed and rolled downhill to crush buildings in the city below. Only the right arm remained, upraised in a desperate bid to grasp at the heavens. A pulsing blue light glowed high above, cupped in the palm of that hand.

"Oromor would have you believe that you can control its power."

Ayleth couldn't find the strength to sit up, to turn, to look. She continued to lie there beneath the broken idol even as Odile appeared through the *oblivis,* the train of her heavy silk robes making a gentle susurrus as it dragged across the stone behind her. She stood over Ayleth, gazing down at her for some moments, then knelt beside her in a pool of dark skirts. Ayleth didn't have to look to know that the hundreds of small wounds she'd dealt had healed. They'd never existed in the first place.

"It's all a deception," Odile said. *"A temptation. It wants you to come find it—not here, but in the waking world. It wants you to take it before I can reach it. It knows you are of my blood. It knows your mortal body can survive its power. But Oromor also knows that it can control you."*

Ayleth shuddered deep in her spirit. It was too horrible, too strange, to lie there listening to the voice of Dread Odile. The Witch Queen, the Poison, the Scourge of Perrinion. To hear her speaking in so calm, so reasonable a voice, like a patient grandmother to a willful child.

"Only one being can control Oromor," Odile continued,

folding her hands neatly in her lap. Her face was as serene as a porcelain mask, her eyes ringed in dark streaks of *oblivis* like carefully applied cosmetics. *"Only its twin—Irimir. My own shade. Even then, the difference in strength between the two is so slight, the smallest imbalance will tip the scales. To wear the* eitr *crown is to walk the very brink of damnation."*

Ayleth didn't want to meet that gaze. She resisted for as long as she was able but felt the compulsion drawing her like a force of nature. At last she gave in, allowing her eyes to flick to one side, to look up into that face so strangely familiar. They studied each other long and hard, and Odile's mouth moved slightly, the barest hint of a smile.

"Do not covet Oromor's power," she said softly, her tone traced with chiding. *"Do not desire the lies it offers. The crown is my burden, not yours. My great and terrible destiny."*

Ayleth's body felt numb. Though all of this was only a projection, her mind told her that the fall she'd experienced broke every bone in her skeleton, so she couldn't move. At least she felt no pain. Or if she did, it was so great that mortal sensations simply couldn't perceive it. Just as the music of the Evanderian pipes was inaudible to mortal ears.

At last, summoning what strength remained to her, she whispered, *"Was it worth it?"*

Odile tilted her head to one side.

"This great and terrible destiny of yours . . . was it worth my mother's death? And mine?"

Silence shimmered in the air between them, thick as floating motes of *oblivis*. Odile didn't break Ayleth's gaze, didn't move, didn't breathe. But her dream form seemed to wilt. The change was almost imperceptible at first—the skin sagging beneath the eyes, around the mouth, along that slender, scarred neck. The raven-black hair fell limp around her face, strands of gray appearing like veins of silver in stone.

At last her thinned lips parted, and she spoke again: *"When they stretched me out across that block, when they held my arms fast and exposed my neck to the blade—when the song of the* Cravan Druch *fell from my lips, activating the spell—all I wished for was death. I craved it. More than anything you can possibly imagine. I saw the faces of my darlings before my eyes. I saw my two daughters—Olena, long dead; Olecia gone. Damned, perhaps. And I longed for nothing more than to join them."*

She bowed her head. Her hair was almost entirely silver now, and her back hunched, delicate shoulder bones protruding like wings through paper-thin skin.

"*But if I died . . . what would become of my people? Of the shade-taken who looked to me for protection? What would become of my city, the haven I had carved into existence with my own two hands? So many would suffer. The possessed would be branded as witches, hunted down and filled with poison. The inborn, tied to stakes and burned for their own salvation. All those suffering souls, without hope, without help.*

"*I alone offered them succor. I alone, with the twinned powers of Irimir and Oromor united, could protect Dulimurian and protect them. But if this host body died, what then? Even if my spirit escaped and found a new host, I would never again wear the* eitr *crown. No . . . no.*" She shook her head, the curtain of silver hair wafting softly like the trailing boughs of a willow moving in a breeze. "*This body must be saved. At all costs, at any cost. This wretched life which meant so little to me . . . but everything to my people.*"

A bitter taste filled Ayleth's mouth. Her lips twisted; her nostrils flared. "*To make your curse work, you had to protect yourself. You couldn't let my mother live. Or me.*"

Odile lifted her head, her hair falling away so that she could look at Ayleth once more. *"It's true. I sent my Crimson Devils to kill you both soon after you were born. It was the only way to make certain the Cravan Druch would sustain me. But Olecia . . . my brave and beautiful daughter, escaped with you in her arms."*

For an instant, she was silent, her lips quivering. But the words slipped out at last, like sparks of fire in the night: *"When they cut off my head, when they burned me and desecrated my mortal frame, I thought of you and your mother. When they laid me out on that cold slab in that crypt black as hell, I saw your faces over and over again. My darlings. My beloved. And how I hoped that you had both lived, that all my plans had come to nothing. I hoped that you would return and kill me once and for all."*

Her face melted into an expression of such mortal pain and love and longing that Ayleth's spirit responded with a painful lurch. She knew she should feel nothing but horror when she looked into that face. But . . . but now other knowledge filled her head. Images of the history Odile had shared with her. Images, memories of triumphs and heartaches. She saw again the young venatrix on her knees in the middle of a burned circle, weeping, screaming, burying her hands and face in the cold ash until she was covered all over, gray as a ghost.

Ayleth shook her head and squeezed her eyes shut. "*A little late for second-guessing, don't you think?*"

Odile was silent for some while before answering. "*I saw the Goddess's hand raised against me. I was mighty, beyond all imagining—but I was not divine. I was not eternal. I saw Her raise Her instrument to bring me down. Her Chosen King, Her promised champion. And I asked myself, 'Do I bow my head to the chopping block? Do I give in to the inevitable divine?'*"

Though she tried to resist the urge, Ayleth opened her eyes and met the queen's gaze. She found herself caught and held fast by the intensity of Odile's soul.

"*I arrived at an answer. And I acted,*" Odile said, her voice full of ugly bitterness. Then it melted into tones of such tenderness as to melt the hardest heart. "*I've had many years now, child, to consider whether my choice was right. Many years of pain . . . and regret.*"

Ayleth couldn't speak. The words seemed to have dried up in her throat. She could only gaze into those black-as-night eyes and feel the connection irresistibly binding the two of them. A connection stronger than any soul tether shared between mortal spirit and shade. The connection of blood kin, which she'd never felt before.

No . . . no, that wasn't true . . .

Her mind flashed with images of her wolf brothers and wolf sisters. Her mother, housed in a wolf's body. She felt again the likeness she once shared with them even though her mortal body was so different from theirs. She hadn't realized the difference at the time, child that she was. Even now, as she gazed back on those newly reclaimed memories, she could scarcely feel it.

This was what it meant to have family. This was what it meant to belong. Not like she belonged to Hollis— Hollis, who took her in only to manipulate and control her, to lie to her. Not like she belonged to the Order— the Order which used her and, when it perceived no further use for her, discarded her. This was a belonging as inborn as her own shade. A belonging of blood to blood.

She belonged to Odile. And Odile belonged to her.

Ayleth's spirit bucked, reeled. A sickening protest swelled in her heart, swiftly growing in pressure until it burst from her mouth in a scream. "*No!*" she shouted, then again and again: "*No! No! No!*"

The mental projection of her body vanished, melting away into pure spirit stuff. Unhindered by the limitations of flesh and bone, she bolted up into the *oblivis*-filled sky, streaking away into darkness, into oblivion. Anything to escape that tether, anything to escape that connection, which she feared more than she had ever feared anything in her life. More than she feared the monsters she hunted. More than she feared the flames of the Evanderians. More than she feared the looming eternity of the Haunts. She could not let herself be bound. She must escape, she must—

The weight of mortality crashed down around her as her spirit returned to her mortal frame. She sat for a moment in the darkness inside her head. Then she opened her eyes and looked out at the looming trees of the Witchwood surrounding her.

She was awake.

CHAPTER 5

DARKNESS ROARED AROUND HIM. BUT AN INSTANT later, he gasped a lungful of cool, clear air.

An instant after that, he passed through into darkness again, into chaos so clamorous, so heavy, so fiery that even a mere instant of it was hell. But that instant passed as well, and he breathed again, this time drawing in the tainted air of the Witchwood. Five times he stepped in and out of this world, each time a flash of reality too swift for comprehension, like a succession of blinks that last for small eternities.

The journey ended as abruptly as it had begun, and not a moment too soon. Every cell of his body strained as though his heart, his blood, his limbs, and his soul were ready to burst into a thousand pieces.

Gerard collapsed in the mud of the Witchwood, arms outspread, legs bent, face turned just enough to one side that he could breathe without inhaling slime and rot. He lay as though broken, his gaze unseeing except for dancing, dazzling beams of light and non-light shooting across his burning eyeballs. His ears were deaf to all save the huge, pounding cacophony of silence and screams that didn't fit within his realm of understanding. His senses were alive, seared with pain, and unable to process the world around him.

He couldn't say how long he remained in this state before he began to reclaim some semblance of reason. It was as though his mind had gathered up everything it had just endured, then locked it away in some deep, dark place where he couldn't see it, couldn't remember it. His senses began to revive. First, he felt all the aches in his body, as if he'd been slammed into a wall over and over. Then he smelled the stench of the putrid soil beneath him, strong enough to make his stomach clench and his throat spasm with bile.

Then his ears opened. And he heard a voice: "*No!* No, no, no, I won't let you hurt him!"

He lifted his head. The ground made a sucking sound as his cheek pulled free, and foulness caked his face and neck and dripped down his front as he got onto his knees. Pain shot through his shoulders and back, but nothing seemed to be broken. Moving with care, he turned toward the voice, which had sunk to a low, wordless moan.

Some yards away, the Phantomwitch knelt with her back to him. He spied her through the haze of *oblivis*, her golden hair standing out in the gloom even when dirty and snarled with debris. She knelt at the base of a tree, clutching at its trunk, her hands tearing into the brittle bark and rotten wood. Pus-like sap welled up from the wounds and rolled down over her fingers and arms.

Gerard stared at those white shoulders—Liselle's shoulders, once soft and voluptuous, now covered in red lines as though she had reached behind and clawed at her own back, trying to tear something invisible off her shoulders. Weeping convulsively, her body quaking with each breath, she didn't seem to be aware of Gerard as he got to his feet and unsteadily approached her from behind.

He stopped within arms' reach, uncertain. He had no weapon—his sword had been left behind when the witch dragged him through realities. Even if he were armed, he couldn't imagine raising a blade to harm her. Not now that he had heard that voice fall from her lips once more.

"Fayline?" he spoke softly.

She stiffened. Then, slowly, she turned to look up at him, her face a snarling mask, its expression monstrous. He took an involuntary step back, his heart leaping to his throat. But the next instant, her face sagged, and the expression melted away as another spirit battled for dominance. She slumped, head sagging, and clung to the tree for support.

"Fayline," Gerard said again and knelt beside her. He reached out, hesitated for a breath, then took her hand.

Her body jolted in reaction to his touch. But her fingers wove through his, and she turned to him, her eyes swimming with tears. "Gerard!" she cried and leaned into his chest.

He held her close as she wept. He tried not to think about how easily she could drag him through to the Haunts, how instantaneous his death might be, with nothing he could do to prevent it. He tried to think of nothing but Fayline . . . Fayline, the girl he had loved in his boyhood. Fayline, madcap and mirthful, with the bell-like laugh, who could dance the night away like a blossom spinning carefree on a spring breeze. Fayline . . . who was his bride. This may not be Fayline's body he held in his arms, but he felt her soul radiating out from its core. He would know her anywhere, regardless of what form she wore.

At last her weeping subsided. She simply crouched there, clinging to the front of his shirt, pressing her head against his heart like a child in need of comfort. He held her, his cheek resting against the top of her head, his arms squeezing gently, as though—if he could just hold her tight enough, if he could only press her close enough—he could somehow, despite everything, still save her.

But salvation was no longer possible, and they both

knew it. So they simply sat, silent and frightened, holding onto what little remained between them. His body trembled. The ordeal he'd just endured and the poison in his lungs left him weaker now than he'd ever been. And beneath that weakness, his heart pounded with the urgency to get moving, to hasten onward to his destiny. Before it was too late. But he stifled these urges. There was no destiny, no vision, no prophecy. Not in this moment. In this moment, brief though it was, there was only Fayline. And he would be present in this moment with Fayline.

At last she pulled back and looked up into his eyes. Liselle's features crumpled as Fayline's soul gazed out through swimming eyes. "Cerine?" she asked softly.

His throat thickened painfully. Through his mind's eye flashed that white, still face lying on the pillow where he'd left her. So cold, so frail . . . so recently broken by a curse she could not withstand. "She's alive," he said. At least, she had been a few hours ago when Terryn met her in Dunloch. What had become of her and all the castle household since then, he couldn't know. As though to convince himself, he repeated, "She's alive."

"Good." Fayline nodded, and her chin sank to her chest. Liselle's ragged curls fell in curtains on either side of her face. "I . . . I didn't want to kill her, Gerard. Not really."

"I know." Gerard touched her cheek tenderly. Her whole body quivered beneath his fingertips, and his soul twisted with sorrow. He wanted to ask her about Terryn. He wanted to ask what the Phantomwitch had done with his brother. But he feared the answer and couldn't make himself speak the words.

"I . . . I don't know if I can hold on much longer," she whispered. "I am so . . . tired. So thin, so stretched. And they are stronger than I. And angrier."

Gerard nodded slowly. He couldn't think what to say, so he kept his mouth tightly shut. When Inren took ascendancy again, she would kill him. If he had any sense, he should rise, strike this host body down while he could, and make all haste away from here. But what was the point? Even if he could bring himself to raise his hand in violence against Fayline, he had no idea where he was anymore. The vastness of the Witchwood surrounded him. There was no sun overhead, no light, no guiding star to provide any sense of direction. Only more gloom and half-light and poison as far as his eye could see.

Fayline tilted her head, fair lashes fluttering softly. "They always told me you were the Golden Prince. The Goddess's promise come to life." There was no mockery in her words. There may even have been a trace of awe.

But Gerard felt as though she'd struck him a blow to the gut. "Yes," he said, releasing a long breath. "They told me the same story. It's not true."

"No," Fayline answered, shaking her head. "No, I've realized as much. I've seen Dread Odile, the Poison. She is alive. Held together by threads of magic, but alive. And she is going to get her crown. Nothing will stop her, not even the Witchwood itself."

"I will stop her." He didn't speak the words with confidence. But as he spoke them, something happened. Something changed inside him. Perhaps it was only his insanity driving him on to deeper madness. It didn't matter. As the words fell from his tongue, his heart beat a steady rhythm and he breathed with greater ease despite the poison in his lungs.

He gazed unblinking down at Fayline, and her eyes

darted back and forth as she studied his face. "You cannot stop her."

"I will," he answered. "But first I must go to Dulìmurian."

Fayline shook her head viciously. "The City of the New Goddess is no more. It belongs to the crown now. Don't doubt me, Gerard! I've seen it with these eyes. I've seen the wall surrounding the city, a wall of living vines. Even Odile cannot pass. Not yet. She made . . . she made the witch try to carry her through. To *evanesce* beyond the wall. It nearly destroyed us."

The effect of her words was quite the opposite of Fayline's intention. Gerard, listening to her warning, felt his hope revive. "Odile hasn't reached the city?" he whispered. Then again, "Odile hasn't reached the city." He stood, strength returning to his limbs as inspiration fueled his soul. "By the Goddess, there's still time!"

Still crouched in the mud, Fayline stared up at him, shaking her head faster and faster. "No, no, no. Didn't you hear me? You can't get through! No one can. Not even Odile."

"But I will," Gerard answered. "I have seen it, Fayline.

It has to be." He extended a hand and, when she hesitantly took it, pulled her to her feet. She stood close to him, cold, trembling, desperate. Spirits warred behind the pupils of her stolen eyes. But he peered beyond the tumult into her center, looking at Fayline and Fayline alone.

"Can you take me there?" he asked. "Can you take me to the wall?"

She nodded slowly. "It is not far. But I have no anchor planted near enough to carry us there. We will have to walk."

CHAPTER 6

TERRYN STOOD BLINKING INTO THE SHADOWS, TRAPPED IN a formless dream.

It didn't stay formless for long. The darkness seemed to coalesce, transforming into shapes he thought he recognized. Slowly the shapes solidified, and his vision cleared. He saw a series of buildings familiar to him, and he walked down a narrow stone path between those buildings, keeping close to a wall. After a few paces, he realized that he was passing by the granary and making for the stables of Dunloch Castle. Moonlight bathed the stone stable yard lying before him, and there was something familiar about all of this, even about the tension in the air.

When his ears caught the sound of soft footsteps behind him, he ducked quickly into the shelter of the granary doorway and peered out from this hiding place to see a figure approaching. She kept close to the buildings as well, using their shadows to hide herself, but sometimes she could not escape a stray beam of moonlight. The white glow revealed a stern face, dark brows, and long, loose hair.

His throat thickened at the sight of her, and his stomach knotted. Something like an instinct or a memory urged him to move. As though he'd done this before. When she stepped down the narrow path leading between the granary and the other stone outbuilding, he reached out and caught hold of her upper arm, feeling the startled thrill of surprise shoot through her. With a single fluid motion, he swung her around and pressed her into the granary door.

Long red skirts flared out, brushing against his legs.

That wasn't part of this memory—no. It would seem his memories were merging. But for the moment he didn't care. Not while he had her in his grasp, one hand still holding her upper arm while the other covered her mouth, stifling her angry scream. Her breath was hot against his palm, and her eyes glared furiously up at him, like flints striking sparks of anger in the darkness.

Those sparks were enough to ignite a fire in his gut.

He leaned closer, and his nostrils filled with her scent—lye soap and horse and pine and leather. And beneath it, the unmistakable perfume of intoxicating womanhood. When he let his hand fall away from her mouth, she didn't speak. Her lips parted, and she drew short, panting breaths. Her chest rose and fell as though she'd just run a mile. She wore a glorious red ballgown that cut away from her shoulders and exposed the white skin of her bosom. He saw the scar from the long cut Fendrel had made when he purged *oblivis* from her body. Extending down between her breasts, it stood out red and raw against that white skin.

His heart ached at the sight. His hand resting on her bare shoulder slid down so that he might rest gentle fingers on the scar, trailing lightly along its length. She shivered at his touch, and her breath caught. He pulled back and lifted his gaze to meet hers. Her eyes burned still, but the glare had melted away into an altogether different expression. Her parted lips trembled.

Heat pounded in Terryn's veins. He knew the law of Saint Evander. For a shade-taken like him to feel what he was feeling, to give in to the sensations burning in his skin, was an unforgivable sin. He knew that to let his gaze linger on her face, her liquid-dark eyes, her lips, her shoulders, was to let himself stand poised on the edge of a precipice. Once he fell, he could never be saved. He must let her go. He must turn away and flee from temptation as he had been trained.

But he couldn't. He stood bewitched.

His mouth moved. He tried to speak her name. But before his tongue could form any sound, she stood up on her toes and pressed her lips to his. That touch sent a shock like lightning straight to his core.

He let go his hold on her arm and grabbed her by the hair on the back of her head, holding her head in place as he kissed her again and again, turning his mouth first one way then another in a desperate need to find the perfect fit with hers. Her hands, splayed on his chest, slid up around his neck, her fingers heating his skin. With a growl in his throat, he pulled her head back and kissed her cheek, her jaw, down her neck to the place where the scar began in the depression between her collarbones. He felt the delicate flutter of her pulse beneath his lips. Her soft whimper sang in his ears, driving him wild.

Suddenly, his arms were full of fire.

Terryn opened his eyes and saw her face staring up at him through dancing flames. He drew back in horror as her skin blistered, peeled away. Her mouth opened in a silent scream of agony, and flames devoured her dress, blackened her skin. Blue flames.

With a horrified cry, Terryn tried to grab her, tried to pull her free of that blaze. But she slipped through his hands, untouchable, unreachable. He felt the heat on his face, his skin, yet the fire did not burn him, only her. He was totally helpless as she was consumed before his eyes.

Around him the world melted away into a chaos of darkness. The pulse of his own horror churned, crushing his soul like a millstone grinding wheat. He whirled in place, searching for some means of escape, some means of help. But he was alone, trapped, watching Ayleth burn, her silent scream shattering his spirit with its unending anguish.

Suddenly, a brilliant white curtain fell before his eyes. No, not a curtain—a wing. Translucent and shimmering with magic and light, it blocked his vision of the darkness, of the burning, filling his eyes with its purity.

You have the air of the Haunts in your blood, a song-like voice spoke in his ear. *It is poisoning you, body and spirit.*

The Haunts?

Terryn blinked several times, reaching his hands to his head and pulling at his hair. Flashes of memory came back to him—images of reality tearing, of Liselle di Matin stepping in and out of the world. He recalled his fight with the Phantomwitch, his darts flying through empty air. Hands on his throat. The witch had dragged him through a crack in reality. In that instant, he'd known he was done for. She would leave him there, trapped in the Haunts, trapped in an eternity of suffering. And there was nothing he could do to stop her.

Only . . .

Another flash of memory. He recalled Nisirdi's bugling roar. He remembered his light-dragon's claws tearing into the Phantomwitch's soul, holding onto her so that she could not shake herself free. She'd been forced to *evanesce* back into the mortal world, bringing Terryn with her. But not before he'd breathed in a huge lungful of pure *oblivis*.

So, the images he'd just seen—of Ayleth in his arms, of those flames eating into her flesh—were nothing but a projection of his mind. Nothing but the torment of the poisoned air he'd breathed working its influence on his brain.

Terryn pulled himself together, his spirit bracing against the horrors he knew waited just beyond the shelter of Nisirdi's wing. "*What can I do?*" he asked, his voice tremulous. He knew of only one way to purge *oblivis* poison from a compromised body. Fendrel had the skill for it, channeling his Anathema blood-magic to purify the blood by taking the curse into himself and then passing it on to another creature. Terryn had watched him perform the spell on Ayleth only ten days ago. But Fendrel wasn't here.

I can help you, Nisirdi said. *I can burn it out of your blood. There isn't much . . . but it will hurt.*

Terryn shivered. He and his shade had not yet learned how to balance Nisirdi's incredible power with the fragility of Terryn's mortal body. It would be all too easy for the light-dragon to burn him alive from the inside out in his efforts to purge the *oblivis*. But what other option was there?

"*Do it,*" he said.

Nisirdi nodded and drew back its brilliant wings. Terryn once more stared into the churning darkness of a deadly world he now knew was only in his head. He saw Ayleth standing before him in that red ballgown, her dark hair falling across her bare shoulders, her head bowed. She looked up at him.

Flames filled her eyes.

Impulse took over, and Terryn extended a hand to her, reaching for her. But before he could take a step forward, Nisirdi rose behind him, opened its jaws, and shot a bolt of light straight into her face. This time, Terryn heard her scream.

He wanted to throw himself at her, to protect her

from the blast, to shield her from that pain. But Nisirdi placed a restraining claw on his shoulder, holding him back. Terryn sank to his knees under the pressure of that claw and could only watch, horrified, as Ayleth burned away. She screamed and screamed, her hands tearing at the empty air as though she could claw her way free. At last, mercifully, smoke rose around her, blocking her from his sight.

By the time the smoke cleared, by the time Nisirdi swallowed back the burning light, the image of Ayleth was no more. Terryn knelt, not in darkness, but in a broad, bare plain. The once cracked, dry soil now rippled with new green growth stirring in a slight breeze. The sky overhead was still heavy and overcast, but not so heavy as it once was, and Nisirdi's shining glow illuminated the world.

But Terryn couldn't rise. Sweat and tears streamed down his face. He couldn't tear his gaze away from the blackened place in the ground where Ayleth had stood. He knew, he *knew,* Haunts damn it, that it was only a mental projection. But it felt . . . real . . .

Wake up now, Terryn. You are still in danger.

Terryn grimaced at Nisirdi's urging. But he felt the waking world near now, felt the aches in his mortal body. He swallowed hard, his gaze lingering on that place where Ayleth had stood, his ears still ringing with the echoes of her screams. Then, with a curse on his lips, he opened his eyes—

—and found himself staring down a dizzying drop to a black, sluggish river far below.

Terryn drew a sharp gasp of breath. The world spun before his vision, and it took him a few moments to realize the movement he saw was the motes of *oblivis* floating like ash in the air.

He seemed to be caught on the side of a steep cliff, wedged between a broken stump and a rocky wall. Crazed and hazy memories returned to him—memories of the Phantomwitch stepping back into the mortal world and dropping him over the edge of this ravine, determined to end his life one way or another, even if she could not leave him in the Haunts.

Nisirdi stirred inside his head. Terryn grimaced. For the moment, there was nothing his shade could do to help him. This wasn't a situation he could blast himself out of.

He took stock of his body, slowly testing each limb to make certain none were broken. He was battered and bruised all over, and his left shoulder smarted, his arm twisted awkwardly around the stump. His right leg dangled out into empty air, while the other was pinned in such a way as to cut off blood flow. When he shifted slightly, he felt the painful prickles of rushing blood. It hurt, and he had to wait some moments before the sensation passed.

He twisted his aching torso and carefully looked up the cliff. It was a good thirty feet or so up to the ridge, with no obvious handholds or footholds along the way. He looked down again and realized the drop was no more than fifteen feet or so. And the cliff angled slightly, creating a slope he might conceivably be able to slide down. A narrow bank lined the river's edge, just wide enough that he might be able to walk it without setting foot in that black, slimy water.

But where did the river lead? While he was on the subject, where exactly was he?

"A mile," he whispered, grimacing. The Phantomwitch

could only *evanesce* within a mile radius of wherever she had planted her anchor. Therefore, he couldn't be more than a mile away from where he and Gerard had faced the witch—

Gerard.

Terryn's whole body jolted. What had happened to Gerard? He'd left him unguarded, unprotected. Was he still alive? Did Inren kill him? Did she drag and leave him in the Haunts as she'd tried to leave Terryn? Gerard would have no means to defend himself, no means to stop her.

"No," Terryn whispered. Inside his head, however, he screamed, nearly incoherent with rage and despair. No, no, no, no! He had only one job, one purpose: to protect the prince. To protect his brother. To guard Gerard against all the evils of this world and any other. One job, one role, one destiny. And he'd failed. Again and again he'd failed—this time worst of all.

Nisirdi moved inside his head, but Terryn couldn't respond. He tried to pull himself up, suddenly determined to climb to the top of the ravine. He drove his fingers into cracks, ignoring the aches in his limbs. But his hand slipped. The rough stones tore at his leather armor and scraped his face and palms as he slid. He landed hard on the riverbank, his chest heaving with ragged breaths, his shoulders slumped, defeated.

But he couldn't stay like this. He regained his feet and stared up the cliff, his mind whirring with swift calculations as he tried to gauge the best route up, the time it would take. All the while, the truth shouted in the back of his brain, and the longer he stood there, the louder it grew until he could ignore it no longer.

Gerard wouldn't be there waiting for him. If he had any sense whatsoever, he'd run as fast as he could the moment the Phantomwitch vanished with Terryn. If he ran hard enough, he might be able to escape beyond the range of her anchor before she found him.

Knowing Gerard, he'd done nothing of the sort. He'd stayed and tried to face the witch on his own, tried to find some impossible way to rescue Terryn. And for his stupidity, he had died.

But . . . maybe not . . .

"I saw the Witch Queen die." Gerard's voice came back to Terryn. He saw his brother's pale face staring at him through the haze of *oblivis,* his golden eyes hard, unrelenting. "And I was there. I saw how it will happen. Odile will never reclaim the Eitr Crown."

Could it be? Were there forces at work beyond their own paltry efforts to do or die, to thwart the tides of destiny?

Terryn straightened his shoulders and turned his gaze upon the winding, sluggish route of the river along the bottom of the ravine. He didn't know where it would lead him, yet somehow he knew this was the path he was destined to walk. "It's not as if I have much choice," he muttered, glancing up at the steep cliff wall again. A wall he knew he could never hope to climb. If this was the Goddess's will for him, She wasn't particularly subtle about making it known.

"Nisirdi," he said, speaking in his mind.

I am here.

"Stay close. We don't know what we'll find this way."

I am with you, Terryn, his light-dragon responded. *To the end.*

Light warmed Terryn's palms, shining between his clenched fingers. Drawing a deep breath, he set out along the riverbank, first at a stumbling walk, and then, as his strength revived, at a run.

He'd not progressed far before he heard the first sounds of battle ahead and the unmistakable dissonance of magic in the air.

CHAPTER 7

AYLETH STARTED UPRIGHT, GASPING A DEEP BREATH, which she instantly regretted when a choking cloud of *oblivis* poured into her already coated throat and lungs. She coughed, gagged, spat, and took little sips of air, trying not to choke. With every cough, her ribs spasmed with pain.

She felt along her side but couldn't tell whether her ribs were broken or simply cracked. Either way, it hurt. Everything hurt. Her ribs, her arms, her neck, her legs.

Her quilted trousers were torn in a spiral pattern from ankle to thigh. Beneath the tears, the skin was raw and red. That must have happened when the vines grabbed her. Her shirt was also torn around the waist, the skin beneath mottled with ugly bruises.

Drawing another little sip of a breath, she observed her surroundings. She was leaning against a tree trunk, tucked in amid a tangle of exposed roots. Other trees surrounded her, standing so close that their branches inextricably mingled overhead. Not many feet away she saw the broken remains of her beak-faced mask. The calendula petals that had served to filter the air and spare her from the worst of the *oblivis* were scattered in bright yellow array across the mucky black soil of the Witch-wood floor.

Ayleth shook her head, trying to remember what had happened. Flashing images of battle and violence filled her mind. Slowly, slowly, some of the moments clarified. She recalled standing on the oblidite-paved Queen's Highway with Fendrel and Hollis flanking her and other hooded Evanderians on all sides. She remembered monsters descending upon them, tortured spirits trapped in hideous host bodies, poisoned by the Witchwood's evil air.

"Hollis," she whispered. "Kephan, Fendrel . . ." Were any of them still alive?

When she moved to sit upright, the shackles on her wrists clanked. She grimaced down at them. Iron. Fendrel's doing, Haunts damn him. How long had she been unconscious? She peered up through the tangle of branches but couldn't get even the faintest glimpse of the sun. Nothing around her indicated the passage of time. She could have been trapped in that dream for hours. It felt as though she'd lived a lifetime . . . a lifetime of someone else's memories . . .

Odile. Ayleth's jaw hardened. Where was Odile?

She peered into the forest around her. The trees stood tall and silent, their wounded trunks slowly seeping pus, which rolled down to soak into the rotten soil. *Oblivis* drifted in lazy currents of air. She saw no sign of the vines that had grabbed and dragged her here. For all she could tell, she was alone.

Her leg buckled when she tried to push up onto her feet, and her ribs spasmed in protest at any move she made. She very nearly sprawled out among those gnarled roots but managed to lean against the tree for support. The putrid pus sap seeped into her garments. But really, she decided with a shrug, it couldn't make her stink any worse than she already did.

Something shifted—something large, like a boulder—just outside her peripheral vision.

Ayleth turned sharply. A jolt of pain shot through her ribs. She gripped her side, staring into the gloom where she could almost swear she'd seen something. There was no movement now. Nothing but the ever-shifting *oblivis* in the air. She hadn't really *seen* anything, only . . . only felt it. Was it nothing but jumpy nerves?

A shiver raced down her spine as she turned her gaze to the ground closer to where she stood, searching for drag marks. When the vines hauled her here, she must have left some sort of trail in her wake. The oozing soil didn't reveal much, but if she searched, she might find scratches on tree trunks, broken branches and bracken, something that would reveal the path, something she could follow back to the Queen's Highway and the Evanderians . . .

That thought trailed off into dead space. She stood for several moments, thinking nothing, looking at nothing, her face slack. Then her brows drew together in a harsh line.

Why would she go back? Why would she try to find them, try to help them? They weren't her friends; they weren't her comrades-in-arms. They were her captors. They were the ones who had put her in these Haunts-damned irons.

They planned to burn her alive.

Ayleth drew a long breath, little caring how the *oblivis* slid over her tongue and down her throat. She had never in her life felt so utterly lost. The vastness of the Witchwood surrounded her, but its shadows and creeping horrors held no dread for her. Even without Laranta's strength, she knew she could handle herself. She was a huntress; she was a fighter. And if she died fighting, so be it.

But if she ever escaped this forest . . . if she didn't die . . . how was she to live?

The ground shook. Something moved.

Ayleth turned, this time more quickly despite the pain

in her side, and just fast enough to see a shadowy hump settle down heavily through the fog of *oblivis*, maybe ten yards away. It was difficult to see with any clarity, but she thought those were . . . spines. No. She shook her head. No, those were merely broken stumps, branches. She must have imagined—

The hump shifted again, rising and moving with heavy-footed stealth. It was huge, a small, living hill.

It was circling her.

Reacting on instinct, Ayleth reached for Laranta's power. But she found only the wall of iron poison inside her. "Haunts," she whispered and braced herself. Her weak right leg tried to buckle, so she shifted her weight off it, raising her shackled hands. This *thing*, whatever it was, had to be a shade-taken. Nothing but shade-taken could survive in the Witchwood. Which meant it wouldn't like iron any more than Laranta did. She could use it, turn her disadvantage into a weapon.

The thing no longer tried to hide its approach. It took several more ponderous steps, and the *oblivis* fog parted before it. Its massive body hit trees, and they cracked, bent, even broke, their weak and wounded trunks unable to resist its passing. It turned its massive head, and she felt the moment it spotted her.

It was like a huge toad—squat, bulbous, slimy. But the slimy skin was plated over with many jutting scales, which bristled out from its body, creating the spine effect. The eyes were tiny points of green, dripping what at first looked like tears but which burned the *oblivis*-thickened air. Some kind of acid, Ayleth guessed.

Its wide mouth dropped open, and a huge swollen purple tongue lolled out, dragging along the ground, collecting rot and bits of debris. The scales along its back and haunches lifted, and more poison bubbled up from the skin beneath to ooze out in great globs.

Suddenly, the misshapen thing bunched together, its haunches quivering. Ayleth had just time enough to realize it was about to spring. She whipped around behind the tree she'd just been leaning against.

The monster smashed into the ground where Ayleth had been standing. Its massive weight shook the ground, and the tree wavered and groaned, its roots trembling beneath the soil. Ayleth staggered and fell headlong. She twisted as she fell, ignoring the pain bursting through her ribs, and looked behind her.

The monster had no neck, so it turned its whole body to look at her. Its mouth opened, and that swollen tongue shot out. It struck the tree rather than Ayleth and stuck against the trunk. The creature yanked, and the tongue retracted, tearing away bark and wood. The tree cracked, moaned, and fell, its trunk broken in two.

Ayleth dodged the falling branches. Flight instinct temporarily overcame the numbness in her leg, and she hurtled forward. No time to worry about directions, about roads, about destinations. All that mattered was getting *away.*

Something hit the back of her knee hard. Her leg gave, and she fell face-first into the mucky earth. She scarcely had time to pull her head up before she was wrenched painfully backward, dragged across the ground with shocking speed. She didn't have time to think about what was happening, didn't have time to feel pain. She had moments in which to react.

Twisting at the waist, ignoring the protest in her ribs, she brought her hands down sharply, cutting the iron links between them straight into that bloated tongue.

With crisp, almost unreal clarity, she saw the little spines on the end of the tongue, which stuck into the fabric of her trousers, into her skin. Then black blood spurted, stinking with shadow blight.

The monster shrieked. It shook its whole body, lashing its tongue back and forth. Ayleth flew right, left, and right again before the barbs on the tongue broke free and she went flying, lucky not to end up brained against a tree. Without Laranta's power ascendant, she had no unnatural strength to protect her. She hit the ground hard, tumbled, landed on her back, and stared up at a canopy of distant branches and a vortex of whirling *oblivis*.

The ground quaked beneath her. Ayleth rolled with no idea where she was going, only certain she'd better keep moving. She rolled until she hit the trunk of a tree and stopped, her hands splayed out before her face, gripping at the black muck.

The end of that huge, purple tongue, trailing blood, struck the ground just inches from her right hand. She jerked back, pushed up onto her knees, rose, staggered, fell, and regained her feet. Whirling, she faced the monster, which loomed over her, massive and hideous beyond imagining. She met its beady, poison-dripping eyes. It opened its mouth, a noxious breath seeping out through its wide, lipless smile.

Its tongue shot out, stuck in the center of Ayleth's chest, and pulled.

Ayleth flung up both hands to grab hold of the top of that ugly mouth. Her feet hit the bottom jaw, and she braced herself, screaming and screaming. With Laranta's strength, she could have broken its jaw then and there, cracked its head wide open. But she had nothing but her own mortal strength—one leg ready to give out, and a torso spasming with pain. Slime and poison surrounded her, and she gazed down into a gulping, eager throat.

Then, before her wide eyes, she saw a cloud of darkness billowing up from the depths of that throat. Darkness that exploded in a burst of power, knocked Ayleth free of the tongue's sticky grip, and sent her flying out of that mouth.

She landed on her back, stunned. Her body was gross with slime, which caught the *oblivis* in the air and coated her entirely. Overhead, more *oblivis* churned, glinting bright with charges of magical energy that even her mortal eyes could see without the help of shadow sight.

Hardly believing she was alive, hardly able to make her lungs draw breath, she rolled onto her side, propped herself on one elbow, and looked back at the monster. It lay in a pile of ruin, a blackened hole blasted straight through its back and out through its mouth. The purple tongue sagged long and limp on the ground, and one misshapen hind leg stuck straight up in the air.

Beyond the shade-taken monster stood a tall, narrow figure dressed in rags. Her hair was long and black, her face as pale as death above a gory neck wound, which was thick with blackened, scabbed blood. Her right hand was still upraised, and *oblivis* whirled around her fingers.

"Odile," Ayleth breathed.

The Witch Queen. Not a figment this time, not a shadow of the mind. In the flesh.

Grimacing, panting, sweat bursting along her brow, Ayleth managed to pull her feet under her. She pressed her shackled hands to her side, half expecting to feel her broken rib protruding through skin and shirt alike. She shook slime from her face, wet strands of hair clinging to her forehead and cheeks.

"All right," she growled. "You found me." She drew herself up as straight as she could, squared her shoulders, and lifted her chin, trying to force any trace of fear from her face. "Go on. Do your worst."

Odile gazed at her over the monster's corpse. Something glinted in her eyes. Tears?

"Olena," she said.

"That's not my name!" Ayleth snarled, spitting blood and slime. "I'm not . . . I'm not some long-lost daughter or granddaughter or whatever the Haunts you think I am. I'm nothing. Nothing but your enemy. I'll kill you if I can. Do you hear me? I'll kill you!"

Odile nodded slowly. She stepped around the monster and approached Ayleth, moving smoothly, almost as though she floated. Perhaps she did. *Oblivis* surrounded her, wafting like a cloak, and possibly carried her so that she need not set foot on that foul earth. Her skin looked snow white against the darkness of the air.

Ayleth's eyes flicked to the blasted monster and back to Odile again. She knew what was coming. Another bolt of *oblivis*, hardened into stone, shooting right through her heart, killing her in an instant.

But Odile closed the distance between them, silent as a specter. Her eyes were round pools of darkness. She nodded slightly, and the *oblivis* set her down as gently as a mother lowering her child to the ground. She stood no more than three strides away.

She raised her arms, spread them wide, and looked Ayleth in the eye. "Very well, my child. Kill me," she said.

CHAPTER 8

FAYLINE HELD GERARD'S HAND AS THEY WALKED through the Witchwood, her steps confident and sure despite the pallor of her face. The moist soil caught at their feet, relinquishing each step with a sucking pop, and their going was slow, uphill most of the way.

The higher they climbed, the farther apart grew the trees around them. Gerard peered up between branches, hoping for a glimpse of clear sky. But he saw only more *oblivis* whirling thickly overhead. He gained no sense of the time of day, though he knew he must have wandered in the Witchwood for many hours now. Soon night would fall, bringing deeper darkness, deeper dread.

Now and then he cast a sideways glance at his companion, at Liselle's lovely profile set in a stern mask. At Fayline's soul shining out from behind those stolen eyes. He did not try to speak to her, nor she to him. What could they say to one another now? Could he bear to apologize again for having left her in the Witchwood all those years? Could he bear to make more excuses, to tell her how everyone had convinced him that her soul was long since lost? Could she apologize for all the death she'd brought upon Dunloch in her madness and jealousy?

They were not the same young lovers they had been on the day of their wedding. Four years may not be much time, but it might as well have been a lifetime. There could be no going back. Not for Fayline, whose body was dead. Not for Gerard, whose heart belonged to another.

But they clung to each other even so, their fingers laced. United for the last time under the shadows of the Witchwood trees.

The landscape rose at a steady incline for a good distance before it suddenly broke off in a huge gash, as though some great beast had taken a bite out of the land. The cliff before them stood at least forty feet high and commanded a view of several miles. Gerard stopped on the edge, his heart pounding as he gazed down at the ruins of Dulimurian, at the distant monolith and the silhouette of the idol, her hand outstretched to the sky. But these could not hold his attention long.

Gerard blinked and took a step back, but forced himself to gaze down, to observe what took place at the base of the cliff.

Monsters more horrific than any a mortal mind could dream up swarmed below, their broken bodies mere cages of wrath to house the spirits burning inside them. They screamed and roared and rattled in a chorus of tortured voices that rent the air and shattered the soul. But even these were not as dreadful as that wall—the living wall of twining black vines that rose to towering heights above their heads. Some of the monsters tried to climb it, but they were quickly caught, dragged inside, and crushed. Bits of bloody, pulpy remains were spat back out again to rain down on the heads of the hellish brethren.

They didn't stop. Their cries unceasing, their ardor undiminished, they threw themselves at the wall, tearing and ripping. Bursts of magic struck the black coils—flames and curses and winds. Sometimes they seemed to make a little headway, and a thin place would appear in the wall, ready to give way. But each time, before the creatures could burst through, the vines reasserted themselves, shooting out to cover the gap and weaving tightly together.

Gerard slowly shook his head. So, this was their temporary ally, was it? The Witchwood itself, fighting against the hordes of Odile, was the only reason their battle wasn't already lost.

"I must get through," he whispered. He didn't speak loud enough for Fayline to hear him. His words were for himself alone. "I have to get through to the city. To the idol." If everything he had seen in Nilly's vision was true, this wall, though formidable, wouldn't hold forever. Odile would break it down, and he must be there on the far side, waiting for her.

He turned to Fayline. She stood close beside him,

trembling like a leaf, staring down at those monsters, at those vines. These sights were not meant for mortal eyes, certainly not for sweet, mirthful eyes such as Fayline's once had been.

Gerard lifted her hand and placed his other hand on top of it, pressing tight, as though he could hold onto her spirit. Startled, she looked up at him. "Can you get me through?" he asked. "Can you . . . can you control your powers? Can you *evanesce*?"

"Not through that." She whimpered, her eyes round and pale in her white face. "I told you, we tried. It nearly killed us."

"Try again." Gerard squeezed her hand urgently. "Please, Fayline. Try again. With me. If we are lost . . ." His voice trailed off, and he shuddered. Those flashing moments of the Haunts were still there in his mind despite his memory's efforts to repress them. To end up trapped in that horror for all eternity was a fate worse than any he could ever have imagined. But he wouldn't be trapped. He couldn't be. Not yet anyway.

He drew Fayline closer to him, close enough that he could lean his forehead down almost to touch hers. "If we are lost, Fayline," he said gently, "we will be lost together."

She whimpered again and bowed her head, closing her eyes against his gaze while monsters screamed and shrieked and died below. Gerard feared she would protest again or simply crumple to the ground beside him. Instead, she reached into the folds of her tattered gown and withdrew a shining black gem. A curse anchor. She began to speak strange words over it in a language Gerard didn't know, moving her fingers in a complex pattern in the air above, as though stitching together invisible threads. It was strange to see. Magic. She was working magic, which he could not perceive without shadow sight but could almost, *almost* feel in the air around them.

At last Fayline crouched and planted the stone into the ground between her feet. She stood up, facing him, and took both his hands in hers. "It is done," she said. "That is my last anchor. If . . . if the Witchwood will not let us through, it should be strong enough to bring us back. But . . ." She didn't finish. And Gerard was grateful for her silence.

He pulled her to him, wrapping her in his arms,

holding her head against his pounding heart. "Fayline," he said, speaking into her hair as she clung tightly to him. "Fayline, I—"

The world tore apart.

Darkness on all sides. Darkness, horror, and his soul twisted and stretched out on a rack. Screams—his own and those of countless others. Ending and endless all at once.

Fayline. Where was Fayline? He reached out with his desperate senses and felt her soul there in his arms. Somehow, he still had physical shape here in this unphysical world as they passed together, following her dark paths.

The last time she dragged him through the Haunts, it happened in only a moment. This was longer. Perhaps two moments, no more. But it felt worse by far. He felt the opposition of a huge, terrible mind thrown against them, ready to batter them back or squash them to nothing. But then, inexplicably, the resistance quickened into interest. It seemed to Gerard as though he heard a voice in his head.

Ah. There you are. I've been waiting for you . . .

Then Gerard was falling, tumbling down hard stone steps. He managed to get one arm up to protect his head, but he could not stop himself until he reached the bottom and rolled onto a flat surface. Every bone in his body rattled, every muscle strained. His skin was a mass of bloody scrapes and bruises. He rolled one last time to flop onto his back and stare up at a distant sky that swirled slowly, heavy with *oblivis*. On the edges of his vision he saw . . .

Towers. Broken structures and arches of black stone. Oblidite.

He sat up, gasping, and looked around. The ruins of Dulìmurian surrounded him—the streets and buildings, the bridges and empty canals. All had been pulled down, broken, and half devoured by the sucking black soil. On the tiered monolith at the city's center, Odile's idol towered over all. Broken, fallen to its knees, headless. Yet still dominating everything in sight.

Something blue glowed in the palm of the idol's enormous upraised hand.

Gerard picked himself up. For the moment, his gaze transfixed, he was unable to look away from the idol.

Then a choking sound caught his ear, and he spun around. "Fayline?" he whispered.

There she was at the top of the stairs. He glimpsed the crown of her golden head as she tried to push herself upright with her arms, but the effort was too great, and she fell flat.

"Fayline!" he cried and hastened back up the steps, staggering all that way. Though his mind and senses were still halfway broken from that journey through the Haunts, he drove onward, determined to reach her.

Before he gained the top of the stairs, she pushed up onto her elbows again and looked down at him. "Stop!" she cried, extending one torn and bloody hand. Then she moaned, her eyes rolling back in her head, her neck drooping forward until her hair dragged on the stones. "It let us through," she said. "It let us through . . ."

"Fayline?" Gerard took another two steps, reaching his hand toward her. "Fayline, it's all right. I'm here."

"I know, I know," she sobbed, her shoulders heaving. "But . . . but . . ." Her face lifted . . . and it wasn't Fayline he saw gazing at him through those stolen eyes. "She's not here, little princeling. Not anymore."

Gerard staggered back, his heart dropping to his stomach. Blood drained from his face, leaving him dizzy, and his vision darkened at the edges. He had no weapon, no means to defend himself.

The Phantomwitch rose upright in sharp, jerking motions, all angles and edges. Her hands curled into vicious claws and her lips pulled back, showing blood-stained teeth. She trembled, staggered, braced herself.

Then she took two lunging steps toward Gerard, ready to grab hold of him, to drag him back to the Haunts and leave him there to fester forever in torment. A hideous laugh burst from her throat as she took a third step.

Before her foot landed, the stone beneath her cracked, and a vine shot from the earth beneath, wrapping up her legs and around her waist, pinning her arms to her sides—coiling thick and fast until she entirely disappeared inside it.

"No!" Gerard shouted. "Fayline!" He flung himself at the coils, tearing at them with his bare hands. But he might as well have torn at stone, so impervious was that fleshy hide. He pounded, swore, pleaded, and wept.

There was a burst of darkness, a rip in the air. An

instant of screaming. Breaking.

Gerard fell to his knees. He couldn't speak. He couldn't breathe. He couldn't think. He could only stare at that vine, at that bulging place where her body should be. He could only watch as drops of blood oozed between the coils to land on the broken stones below.

The vine recoiled, sliding back under the ground. The stone stair rippled with its movement, and then all was still. There was nothing left behind. Nothing. Except . . .

Gerard bowed his head, bowed his whole body to the ground, his teeth grinding so hard he thought his jaw might break. Tears poured down his face, and his frame shuddered and heaved. Then he vomited, and the contents of his stomach were black with *oblivis* dust as they poured out onto the steps below.

Then he crawled, dragging his body heavily to the remains smeared on the stone. Tears clouded his eyes, but not enough to blind him to the horror of that sight. His hand reached out, trembling, and found broken fingers, which he clutched tight.

Fayline . . . Liselle . . .

His lips moved, struggling to form words that would

not come. *"May the Goddess receive you . . ."* He choked, spat, and doubled over. *"May the Goddess . . . may the Goddess . . .* Oh, Goddess!"

He broke with sobs. The whole weight of evil and horror fell on his shoulders. He felt the cruelty, the wrongness, the sordidness that had led them all to this place. He felt his own guilt—all the ways, great and small, in which he had paved this road of horror. The hopelessness, the uselessness, was more than he could bear. He knew he could never stand again, could never find the strength.

A gentle coolness touched his brow, like the brush of a soft hand.

Gerard . . .

His heart froze in his breast. He must be mad. He must have lost his wits.

Gerard . . . my love . . .

He sat up sharply, pulling his head back. His lungs tightened, unable to draw breath.

What was this light shining, unseen by the eyes? What was this voice, this voice he almost knew?

A touch of fingers, featherlight on his cheek. A brush

of lips against his open, sagging, dust-stained mouth . . .

He blinked. And he was alone on the steps, crouched over the sorry remains. Alone with his limited mortal senses. Trapped in his mortal body. Alone.

The silent streets of Dulimurian surrounded him. The idol waited at his back.

Gently, reverently, Gerard laid Liselle's bloody hand across what remained of her breast. With trembling fingers he closed her eyes. He wasn't sure he would have the strength to stand, but when he braced his legs, they obeyed him. He rose, turned. Faced the idol.

Faced what must be his end.

"Goddess," he whispered. "My life, my death . . . whatever remains. Use it."

He began to descend the stair, heading down to the road that led straight through the ruins to the city's center.

A gleam caught the tail of his eye. Gerard looked and saw the bright edge of something lying at the base of the stair, off to the side and half hidden. He'd not noticed it before. But he knew what it was before he even saw it clearly. He moved toward it on an impulse like instinct and crouched to pick it up, his hand closing confidently around the hilt of a sword.

A black sword carved from pure oblidite. Sharper than any steel. He turned it slowly, gazing with no little wonder up and down its length. Its crafting was perfect, the weight of it comfortable and oddly familiar in his hands. A gift fit for a prince. For a king.

Gerard grimaced. He tasted *oblivis* and vomit in his mouth.

CHAPTER 9

ODILE'S WORDS RANG IN THE AIR, ECHOING LIKE distant shrine-house bells:

Kill me.

Kill me.

Kill me.

Ayleth stared at Dread Odile. Her vision seemed to darken around the edges, tunneling into perfect focus on that tall, cold image. The echoes died away, leaving behind a silence so perfect, so complete that Ayleth almost believed she could hear the whisper of the *oblivis* motes as they churned in the air.

A sudden, savage yell erupted in her throat. Ignoring the pain in her ribcage and leg, she threw herself straight at Odile, catching her by the throat. She didn't need Laranta's strength, not then, not in that wild moment of bloodlust. Her own body was empowered enough. She tossed the witch down as easily as a straw doll. Odile smashed into the oozing black soil, foul mud staining her face and splashing up into Ayleth's eyes. Ayleth sank down on top of her chest, sitting astride her, and slipped the iron chain of her shackles under the woman's chin, against her throat, pressing hard, and harder, right along the hideous scar left when the Chosen King cut off the Poison's head.

Ayleth didn't need ascendant shadow senses to feel the mounting power of magic around her. The spirit inside Dread Odile responded to the attack, lashing out with dark, shadowy arms. But though Ayleth could feel the magic brimming up around her like a storm, no blow came.

Instead, a weird song rang in her ears. Like the song of

an Evanderian pipe but more complex, more terrible. A song which, she realized, had been there all along, only she couldn't hear it until now. Only in this moment—this moment balanced on the edge of life and death—did it become audible, cutting past her limited mortal senses to strike her suppressed shadow senses.

She'd never heard a song quite like this, yet she recognized at once what it must be. It couldn't be anything else—for this song was made of death screams and terror, of flowing blood and frightened souls, of pain and sorrow and tears and wretchedness, all blended into a terrible chorus of a thousand keening voices.

This was the *Cravan Druch*. The song spell sustaining Odile's life.

The spell which only Ayleth could break. The spell she was breaking.

Ayleth firmed her jaw and redoubled her efforts, pressing harder with that chain. Her fists planted in the mud on either side of Odile's neck, and she leaned her full weight into them. Odile's eyes bulged. Her mouth opened; her tongue protruded. Her hands tore at the empty air. She might easily have scratched out Ayleth's eyes, shredded her skin, but she didn't touch her granddaughter.

At any moment the attack would come. Ayleth knew it, braced for it. And it would be a death stroke, sudden, painful, and complete. She'd seen what Odile's shade could do, she knew how powerful it was. The *oblivis* in the air would harden suddenly into a spike and skewer her, pin her to one of the trees. Or the *oblivis* in her lungs would spontaneously ignite, burning her from the inside out. She expected these and many other horrible deaths.

But Odile's shade, though thrashing wildly in torment, didn't attack.

Was it the iron? Was the shade reacting so strongly to the touch of iron against its host body's throat? But no . . . such a small amount of iron couldn't subdue so great a power. No, it couldn't be that. It could only be . . .

Odile herself. She held her shade at bay. She would *let* Ayleth kill her.

The *Cravan Druch* swelled to a feverish pitch.

With a guttural gasp, Ayleth lifted her hands and fell back, pushing with her feet to scoot away from Odile's prone body. She backed all the way into a tree and pressed her shoulder blades into its trunk, panting wildly. She didn't know why. She didn't understand it. Haunts damn it, she should finish the job! She was so close . . . She whimpered, pressing her hands to her heart. Tears streamed from the corners of her eyes and raced down her cheeks.

Odile lay still for some time. Only the convulsive rise and fall of her chest indicated life. Then, slowly, she sat up. *Oblivis* whirled around her, pulling the muck and mud from her hair and peeling it from her skin, cleansing her until she was as pure and pristine as a lady fresh from the baths. Her black hair fell in waves around her face, over her shoulders. She looked hardly any older than Ayleth herself. But her neck wound was raw and ugly. The scar had reopened a little under Ayleth's attack

Odile put her hand to her throat, fingers sliding gently up and down. She turned to Ayleth, regarding her mildly. "You've not quite finished, child. Would you care to try again?"

Ayleth couldn't answer, not even to shake her head. Her whole body quaked, though she didn't understand it. Was it a spell? Some protection, some variation of the

Cravan Druch? Something to keep her from accomplishing her purpose?

No. She knew the truth. She couldn't do it. She *could not* kill Dread Odile. Not because of a spell or magic or suppression. This was nothing but her own weakness, her own fear. She could not bear to do it.

Because then . . . she would be truly alone in this world.

In her mind she saw the images of the dream again— of Odile with her hands buried in ash, face lifted to the heavens as she screamed—of Odile lying in a birthing bed surrounded by dark curtains as a midwife tucked her daughter, Olecia, into her arms—of Odile standing high in the palm of her mighty idol's hand, watching the approach of the Chosen King's army, watching the fall of Cró Ular in the distance.

Odile alone.

Ayleth blinked and the vision vanished. She was once more in the Witchwood, her back pressed against a wounded tree. She met Odile's gaze. The Witch Queen already stood, her hands absently arranging her tattered robes around her slender body while she regarded Ayleth with a gentle expression. Then she put out her hand.

"We need not be alone anymore now that we have found one another."

Ayleth shuddered, staring at that hand. She thought of Hollis kneeling before the little feral girl in the forest. She thought of dead wolves lying slain in a circle of firelight around her. She desperately tried to recall all that she knew—all those stories Hollis had told her. The atrocities committed by this woman, this demon. The slaughter of innocents, the torment of mortals, the ravaging of lands and temples and libraries.

But were any of those stories true? Or, if they were true, did they undo the deeper truths Ayleth now knew? The truths of Odile's origins, her goals, her desires. Her sacrifices.

Ayleth couldn't tear her gaze away from that hand. She felt the compulsion come over her, burning in her breast. Or was it merely the *oblivis* she had breathed? Was she succumbing to its poison? Odile controlled *oblivis,* and she could exert control over those who inhaled it as well. Perhaps none of these impulses now warring in Ayleth's brain were her own. They might be nothing more than the witch's manipulations.

Ayleth dragged her eyes up to Odile's face. Her mouth moved several times before she could find the strength to speak. "Why don't you kill me?"

It was a good question. If the laws of the *Cravan Druch* held, then Ayleth was the only thing standing between Odile and true immortality. No one could touch her; no one could kill her. Only one of her own blood. Only Ayleth, her last remaining kin.

Ayleth crouched like a fawn at the mercy of a lion. There was nothing she could do to save herself, nothing at all.

But Odile tilted her head to one side, her face melting into an expression of sorrow and compassion. "Do you still not know?" she said in a voice that would break the hardest heart. "Do you still not understand? My heart, my soul, my little love. I would rather die at your hand than live another day without you by my side. Please, Olena, please, my darling—if you will not take my hand, then finish what you set out to do. Kill me now. Let me join your mother in the Haunts, and we will await your coming there."

It couldn't be true. It had to be a trick. All those memories planted in her mind . . . had followed this convenient rescue from a deadly monster. It was a game designed to lower Ayleth's guard, to make her vulnerable.

But . . . why?

That hand remained in the space between them, extended in gentle offering. Ayleth looked at it again, feeling once more the compulsion to take it.

"Come with me, my love," Odile said. Her voice quavered as though she fought to suppress an upswelling of intense emotion. "We will go to Dulimurian together. Reclaim our kingdom and rebuild. We will summon the shade-taken to shelter with us. All of them . . . all those whom the Order of Evander would see dead. They will live safely under our protection, yours and mine."

Terryn.

She shouldn't have let herself think his name. But there it was in her mind, undeniable. Terryn . . . who would be hunted down by the Order and killed as a heretic. Terryn . . . who would spend the rest of his life in hiding, fleeing those who were once his brethren.

Unless . . . unless . . .

Could there be such a place, such a world, where people like Terryn could live in peace? Where a vision like the one she had glimpsed in the dream could come to pass? She and Terryn together, free, their own inborn children clasped in their arms and their shades ascendant, unfettered, and glorious. A world of true grace and magic and beauty.

Hollis had told her stories of Dulimurian. Of the horrors and atrocities committed there under Odile's rule. But Hollis was an Evanderian. And Hollis needed Ayleth's wholehearted devotion. She had needed Ayleth to believe every word she told her so that when the time came, she would strike her deadly blow without hesitation or question.

Hollis had lied.

"Sweet girl," Odile whispered, "take my hand. Walk with me a little. I can show you a world unlike anything you've ever known. But it will be a cold, hollow world without you by my side. So take my hand, Olena. Take my hand, my love."

Her spirit trembled to its core. Down beneath the iron suppressions, Laranta howled and protested and raged . . .

but her voice was distant, so faint.

Ayleth gazed into those eyes that were mirrors of her own. Into that face, that likeness she had inherited. Into that soul so akin to her own. In one last desperate attempt to resist, she moved her lips, trying to remember one of the prayers Hollis had taught her over the years. None came to mind, not a single phrase. She whispered only, "Goddess . . ."

Then she slipped her hand into Odile's and allowed the Witch Queen to pull her to her feet.

"Come then," Odile said when they stood face-to-face, their eyes at the same level. "Come home to Dulimurian."

CHAPTER 10

A DISTINCT UPWARD SLANT TO THE QUEEN'S HIGHWAY made the going difficult. Hollis heard heavy breathing through the masks around her—even Fendrel, walking at her side, breathed hard—and her own lungs heaved with difficulty. *Oblivis* coated her tongue. The calendula petals weren't helping much anymore. If they'd ever done any real good in the first place.

She kept her shade senses keen, searching the forest on all sides for telltale signs of another spirit approaching.

Much of her awareness focused ahead, watching for any sign of Venator Kephan. He was currently several lengths ahead of the rest of them, using his Feral abilities to scout out what lay ahead.

Hollis had played her Vocos again, lengthening her shade's soul tether, which allowed her to reach through its powers for nearly half a mile all around. It communicated its findings to her—the taste of the putrid air, the trees' whisperings, the subtle vibrations of magic everywhere around them. All felt strangely still.

Surely, she would feel something. If Odile had reached and reclaimed the Eitr Crown, there would be some distinct change in the atmosphere. Maybe nothing major at first. The Witch Queen would have to remaster those terrible powers, would have to reassert her control over the possessing spirit within the *eitr*. Even then, she would probably choose to act with subtlety at first. It wouldn't be wise to overextend herself so soon after her reanimation.

But . . . no. Hollis shook her head, dismissing these thoughts as foolish. She knew Odile too well to believe them. As soon as that crown was on her head, she would shred this entire forest, pulling up every tree and vine by its roots. The fact that the Witchwood still stood was proof enough that Odile had not yet reached her goal.

There was still time. There was still a chance.

A burst of sensation rippled along her shade's soul tether. Wincing, Hollis stopped short. Fendrel halted, giving her a questioning look, and the two young venators behind them crowded in close.

"Magic," Hollis growled. "A . . . a storm of magic. Up ahead."

"Kephan?" Fendrel asked.

Hollis shook her head. She couldn't say anything for certain. "It's . . . big," she whispered.

The young venator snapped his scorpiona into firing mode. Hollis felt ripples in the air from unsuppressed shades pulling at their tethers, eager to fight, eager to let loose their powers. The young venatrix gasped sharply as though in pain.

"You," Fendrel said, turning to the girl, his brow stern and hard. "Use your Vocos. Suppress that spirit."

"But," the girl panted, her eyes wide behind her mask, "if I suppress it, what will I do? I don't have enough poisons left, and—"

"You'll be good for nothing if you're fighting your own shade before the battle even starts," Fendrel answered, no trace of sympathy in his voice. "Do what you have to. Now."

The girl looked desperately from Fendrel to Hollis. Hollis knew better than to offer sympathy, to offer softness. A venatrix had to be hard, had to be strong, had to make the tough decisions that no mortal ever should make. She said only, "You can relax the suppressions again before we reach the city."

It wasn't much. But it seemed to bolster the girl's courage. She pulled out her instrument and set to work playing the Song of Suppression, a subtle variation intended to lightly rein back the Anathema she carried. It resisted, fighting so hard against those restraints that the girl staggered a few steps and almost lost the line of music. But she braced herself, played a more vicious variation, and forced more of her shade's powers down deep.

When her song ended, the girl folded and sheathed her Vocos. To Hollis's shadow sight, she looked strangely frail now with only the barest traces of her powers still accessible. If they were attacked again, she would be targeted by the shade-taken creatures as vulnerable. They would kill her within moments.

Hollis glanced Fendrel's way. But she knew as well as he did that there was no other help to be offered. His mouth was a grim line. "Come," he said.

Hollis reached out with her shade, lightly touching the edge of the young venatrix's mind. Nothing but fear there, pure fear. Hollis quickly pulled back, her heart shivering. But perhaps fear was what the girl needed. Perhaps fear would quicken her reflexes, help her stay alive.

A humming vibration sounded in the air, stirred to life by the many wings of Hollis's shade. At this signal, Hollis's attention snapped forward. "Kephan is coming," she told Fendrel.

He grunted in response and lifted one hand to signal a halt. They stood, weapons raised, mortal senses alert, shadow sight straining, and waited, watching the road ahead. Was it Hollis's imagination or did thickening *oblivis* fog obscure the road? Night must be coming, an end to this interminable day. But when darkness fell, what end would it bring?

"Dominus?"

Kephan's voice sounded through the fog. He appeared a moment later, his Feral shade glowing bright in his eyes. He hastened toward them, breathing hard, his face flushed.

"Report," Fendrel said.

Kephan snapped a smart salute, but his words spilled out almost too quickly to be understood. "The shade-taken—the shade-taken of the Witchwood—so many of them, more than we thought! They're ahead, at the end of this road."

"A trap?" Hollis asked, her voice thin and tight through her mask's beak.

Kephan shook his head. "I don't think so. There . . . there's a wall. Like the one I described earlier, the one I found when I followed Ayleth's trail. A wall of vines, but . . . but so much bigger than the last one! It's huge and extends for miles on either side. It might surround the whole city; I can't say for certain. It's the Witchwood. It's . . . it's keeping them out."

"That's good," said the young venatrix at Hollis's shoulder. "Isn't it? It means the Witch Queen can't have gotten through."

Fendrel ignored her, his gaze intent on Kephan's face. "What of Odile? Did you see her?"

"She's not there. Not that I could detect."

Hollis's heart went cold in her chest. If Odile wasn't with her horde, where was she? "What about the Crimson Devils?" she asked. "Any sign of them?"

"No," Kephan said. "Just the shade-taken. The monsters. They're killing themselves trying to tear down that wall. I would guess they're under compulsion, though I don't know for certain."

With as much *oblivis* as the beasts had breathed over the years, they would be highly susceptible to Odile's will. She must have compelled them to tear down that wall. But why she didn't stand by to watch their progress, Hollis didn't like to guess.

She thought of Ayleth out there in the wood somewhere. Alone. Frightened. Vicious and determined. Would she come? Would she pour all the dogged determination Hollis had seen in her over the years into this last great hunt? Was she even now hot on the Witch Queen's trail?

"What will we do, Dominus?" the young venatrix asked. The venator at her side echoed her question, and they all looked to Fendrel. Even Hollis.

Fendrel met her gaze and held it. But he spoke to Kephan. "Will the horde get through?"

"It's hard to say," Kephan replied. "The wall is strong. The magic coursing through it is unlike anything I've ever encountered. But . . . there are so many of the shade-taken. And Odile's will is a force to be reckoned with!"

Fendrel's mouth curled at the corner in a facsimile of a smile. "What do you say, Venatrix di Theldry?" he asked, still looking at Hollis. "You are the one who declared your intention of marching on Dulimurian. Will you march still?"

"I will," Hollis answered and raised her scorpiona so that the metal fastenings flashed. "If there is even a chance the horde can break through, I will defend that wall."

Fendrel's smile grew. "There you have it." He turned to the others, sweeping his arm in a grand gesture. "We have a plan. The five of us against countless shade-taken. It will be the stuff of legends."

The pale venator and young venatrix exchanged glances. For a moment Hollis expected them to protest, to deny the will of their dominus. To turn on their heels and flee. She'd seen hunters of greater experience turn back in the face of Odile's armies in the days of the Witch Wars, during the campaigns of the Chosen King.

But these two had come this far and endured so much. They were no cowards.

"For the king," said the venator, pressing his left fist to his right shoulder.

"The Golden King," said the venatrix, echoing her hunt brother's salute.

Kephan cursed softly. Then he raised his fist as well, Feral light glowing in his eyes.

Without a word, Fendrel turned and strode on up the road's steep incline, nearly vanishing into the *oblivis* fog. Hollis hastened after, and the others followed at her heels. She heard the young venatrix's Vocos pipes singing as the poor girl once more loosened the suppressions on her shade.

CHAPTER II

AYLETH FELT THE TENSION OF THE WITCHWOOD beneath her feet. The ever-present heartbeat was quicker than before.

Boom-boom . . .

. . . boom-boom . . .

. . . boom-boom . . .

Oblivis thickened in the air, drawing in closer until the floating motes were a thick, dense wall that blocked off all sight beyond a three-foot radius. The only remaining means of measuring either distance or time was footsteps, and Ayleth had long since lost track of those.

She walked a step or two behind the tall, spectral figure. A majestic figure straight out of childhood tales of monsters and nightmares, an image of absolute terror . . . and Ayleth felt as though she may have been walking there all her life. As though every moment of her existence had led to this place, as though the very blood in her veins had destined her, from the day of her first breath until now, to walk in the shadow of Dread Odile.

Boom-boom . . .

. . . boom-boom . . .

. . . boom-boom . . .

The thickened *oblivis* was Odile's doing, no doubt. Had she summoned the element as a shield around them, protecting them from the Witchwood's gaze, from the Witchwood's malice? Or—a small part of Ayleth's mind protested despite her wish to keep it silent—or did Odile keep the air thick so that Ayleth could not help but breathe it in and therefore remained susceptible to manipulation and control?

No. Ayleth's jaw tightened, and her shackled hands

clenched into fists. She was under no one's control. Though she felt the thick layers of *oblivis* clog her throat, she retained command of her senses, her decisions. If she chose to walk with the Witch Queen for the moment, that was *her* choice. She was simply watching for the right opportunity, waiting for . . .

Her eyes moved in their sockets. From her angle just behind Odile's right shoulder, she could see the queen's pale profile, the line of her chin and neck. And the hideous gash where her head had been severed. Ugly finger-shaped bruises were visible around that gash, and patches of raw skin where the iron of Ayleth's shackles had bit deep.

She had been so close. So close to ending the Poison. So close to fulfilling Hollis's intended purpose for her. So close to being the tool the Evanderians needed in this fight. So close . . .

Odile turned her head just slightly, her gaze moving to meet Ayleth's. Ayleth looked away quickly, staring down at her hands. A shudder rippled up her spine and burst like spreading frost in the back of her brain. Could Odile read her thoughts? Ayleth grimaced. Helplessness and hope twisted in her gut like twin writhing snakes.

"Can you get these off?" she asked suddenly. Her voice sounded oddly smothered and soft in that thickened atmosphere. Summoning her courage, she met the Witch Queen's gaze again. At the questioning lift of Odile's eyebrow, she lifted her hands to display the shackles and the links of iron chain.

Odile paused, considering the question. Then she shook her head. "I'm afraid even *oblivis* is of little use against iron." She turned again, her black hair and tattered garments sweeping behind her, and continued her purposeful pace. How she could walk in this gloom with such confidence seemed a miracle in itself to Ayleth. Odile did not depend on mortal senses to guide her to her destination. "When I have my crown," she said, tossing the words back, "it will be nothing for me to break your chains. Then, I swear, you will never be bound by iron again."

Ayleth clenched her teeth, biting back the retort that sprang to her lips. Was Odile telling her the truth? Or was this another manipulation? She'd seen what the Witch Queen could do with the power of her single shade. She'd seen the forest of petrified oblidite. Iron was a unique substance in the world, strangely resistant to magic and repellent to shades. But it was difficult to believe that, with all the power she commanded, Odile couldn't break a few small links.

Was it simply that she didn't want Ayleth to have access to Laranta?

Maintaining her pace a few steps behind Odile, Ayleth reached down inside herself, searching for Laranta. Her wolf shade had given her so much that day, fighting against the iron influence to offer Ayleth all the strength, all the magic she could give. She was exhausted now, severely suppressed. Feeling along their soul tether, Ayleth could just sense her shade quivering deep down near her core. She couldn't conjure up a mental image of her wolf. The iron had obscured even that, leaving only a faint impression of formless spirit deep, deep down.

"*Laranta.*" Ayleth whispered the name inside her head, afraid to speak out loud. But she couldn't leave her shade without some word of comfort. "*Laranta, I swear . . . if I ever get out of these chains, I will never allow anything to separate us again. Not iron, not poison, not fire, not death. Not the Haunts themselves."*

Did Laranta hear her? Did she feel the truth humming deep in Ayleth's own spirit? Did she understand? But of course she did. For they were of one mind, one spirit, bonded at birth, inborn and inseparable. Not even the lies Ayleth had believed over the years had been able to sever the love between them.

For, yes, Ayleth knew without the faintest shadow of doubt that Laranta loved her. Perhaps not in the way that mortals understood love, for Laranta was not mortal. She existed beyond the limitations and confines that structured a mortal's understanding of life and love. But her love was no less profound for being mysterious.

Was it true that such a being was an abomination in the eyes of the Goddess? If so, then Ayleth must be an abomination as well, for she would allow no fire to separate her from her shade. Where Laranta went, she would go as well. If that meant the eternity of torment awaiting them in the Haunts, so be it. Ayleth would never send Laranta to face that fate alone.

Boom-boom . . .

. . . boom-boom . . .

. . . boom-boom . . .

The heartbeat of the Witchwood grew so loud, so insistent that it jarred her out of her thoughts and back into the world in which she walked. The ground vibrated beneath her feet, and the trees around her seemed to move up and down in a pulse like breathing, their roots scrabbling to keep a grip on the rotten soil.

Ayleth stopped. Her mortal senses shivered in reaction to something . . . something not quite a sound. If only she had access to her shadow senses, she knew she would feel powerful magic in the air. A shudder of dread shot through her body.

Odile, who had progressed several paces ahead and was nearly hidden from view in the *oblivis* atmosphere, stopped and looked around at Ayleth, reading her face. Her stern features momentarily flickered with unease. "The crown," she said. "It feels my approach. It seeks to prevent my return to Dulimurian. It has raised defenses, and my servants seek to tear them down." She extended a hand to Ayleth. "Come. We must join them."

For a moment Ayleth couldn't move. Then she nodded and stepped forward. But she didn't take Odile's hand.

The landscape was rough and broken in this part of the Witchwood, with sudden drops into deep gorges and equally sudden rises that never quite reached open sky. It ought to have been slow going, but the *oblivis* seemed to gather under Ayleth's feet, and while she never quite felt as though she was floating, she did suspect that it carried her along faster than she would have moved on her own. Odile progressed ahead of her, every movement gliding and smooth, betraying not the least sign of haste. Only her hair flying out behind her betrayed her actual speed.

Suddenly a cliff at least fifty feet high dropped away before them, appearing in the mist as though from nowhere. Wounded trees gripped its rim, jutting out at bizarre angles, contorted in their efforts to keep hold. The cliff face itself was sheer rock with no growth down its side, and Ayleth commanded a clear view of the landscape sweeping below her.

For the first time, she saw Dulimurian. She saw the outermost rings of the city, the devastated streets and buildings of oblidite sunk into the rotten earth, pulled apart by relentless vines. She saw the roads caved in, the bridges fallen, the canals sunken and dry. Destruction everywhere . . . and yet, somehow, magnificence remained.

In the distance—not such a great distance now, probably no more than two miles—stood Odile's mighty idol on its monolith in the center of the city. Even headless, even brought to its knees, it towered over Dulimurian and the surrounding wood, its one arm outstretched to the sky. Between the pillar fingers, something glowed. A pulsing blue light, hypnotic in its luring beauty. When she dared to lift her gaze to that glow, Ayleth found herself unable to think, feel, or observe anything else, captured as she was by that single pinpoint of light. Her soul seemed to stretch out from inside her mortal body, drawn toward the living *eitr* and the Presence that possessed it.

A terrible shriek ripped the air below, and the sounds of battle sliced through her senses, drawing her back into herself. Ayleth blinked, took a half step back, and looked down to the stretch of ground below the cliff.

The five Evanderians reached the top of the rise where the ground broke and gazed into the valley below. They saw the nightmare horde just as Kephan had described it, flinging itself against the Witchwood's wall, breaking like waves only to regroup and attack again.

Hollis slotted a Gentle Death into her scorpiona and looked to her right, catching Fendrel's gaze again. "Are you ready?" she asked with a smile.

They wouldn't survive this. None of them would.

The smile he returned to her was like the flash of a knife. Then he turned and faced the monsters, faced the hopeless end before him. A wild battle cry burst from his throat as he leaped and skidded down the rough slope a good thirty feet to the ground below, where he landed on his feet in a deep crouch. His powerful legs propelled him up and into the shade-taken ranks almost without pause. A ravening thing flung itself at him, and he took it down with a Gentle Death before lashing out with a blood curse that slaughtered three more in a gory wave of magic.

Hollis's shadow senses exploded with spirits loosed from their mortal dwellings. Her soul trembled as the air overhead ripped and the Haunts opened wide to claim their dues.

Then she too was leaping, sliding down that steep incline without waiting to see if the others followed. This was not a battle that could be fought with any synchronized formation. Each would simply do whatever could be done, alone in the melee of death.

She targeted her shade at the nearest mind and unleashed her powers, the darkest side of her abilities, the side she had tapped into only a few times since her Possession. Her shade lanced into the shade-taken creature's mind and filled it with fear, pure fear, the worst kind of fear—without hope, without escape. Its mortal body stopped its wild run at the wall, standing bolt upright, then began to shake as though the excess of emotion would burst through its pores.

The creature's heart stopped. It crashed to the ground in a tangle of misshapen limbs, dead of fright.

Hollis whipped her shade out of its head and sent it flying into the next shade-taken, the soul tether flashing like a fire-hot whip.

When something loomed at her right, Hollis turned

and shot the Gentle Death straight into a wide, red eye. A haglike woman with the jaws of a beast collapsed in a bundle of bones at her feet. Hollis reloaded while simultaneously commanding her shade. Another monster uttered a howl of pure terror and fell, twitching in its death throes. Hollis raised her arm and took quick aim. Another shade-taken fell before it crashed into her.

It was only then, nearly a full minute into her fight, that she realized . . . the monsters were not fighting back. The compulsion driving them toward the wall was overpowering; they made no move to defend themselves unless something stood directly in their path.

She could use this to her advantage.

Hollis backed up even as she whipped her shade into yet another mind and ended another life in a flash of pure horror. Off to her right she saw a Red Hood, one of her comrades, but she had no time to turn and see which one while loading her scorpiona again. These were terrible deaths she gave—deaths she hated herself for giving. No creature, however maddened with shade blight and curses, deserved to die of fear. But her shade was her greatest weapon. And here, at least, she need not concern herself with gentleness.

Grim-faced, she lashed her power into another mind. But this time it met resistance.

Hollis blinked, staggered, as her shade was flung roughly out into the ether. That was no mind she had entered, not a real mind. Using her physical eyes, she looked at the creature she'd tried to penetrate, a many-jointed, insect-like thing with an all too human face.

It shook its head, dizzy from the attack. Then it turned and fixed its huge, faceted eyes on Hollis. Fifteen other heads turned at the same time. Fifteen identical heads.

"Haunts damn!" she cried. It was a Hive shade—a single entity made up of multiple parts. Only one of the many carried the original mind, the mind she could overcome, and the compulsion didn't seem to distract this creature from its attacker. Perhaps because it had multiple bodies, it could spare a few to deal with this enemy at hand.

Fifteen creatures sprang at Hollis, leaping across the ground in strange, angular bounds, wide jaws clacking with eager rage. Hollis shot one with her Gentle Death, and it fell, but the others were just behind it. She yanked on the soul tether, pulling her shade around her like a shield. But the shade-taken swarmed in, blocking her sight, blocking out all escape. She punched, slashed, cut, stabbed. But there were too many.

Perhaps she imagined it . . . but in the last moments before darkness fell, she thought she heard Fendrel's voice shout her name.

CHAPTER 12

THE RIVER EMERGED SUDDENLY FROM ITS WINDING canyon, falling as a waterfall into a small lake far below. Terryn, relieved to finally escape the walls hemming him in on either side, stepped out to the edge of the waterfall, planting his boots carefully on the slick stones, and gazed into the valley.

Into Dulimurian, the ruinous city. Surrounded by a wall of living vines—a strange and striking sight.

But there was no time to take it all in. For the last mile

he'd been hastening toward sounds of battle and an ongoing reverberation of magic in the air, and now he'd finally found the source. Masses of shade-taken monsters threw themselves into that black, twining wall, tearing at it with their physical bodies and with all the magic they could muster.

"*What is this, Nisirdi?*" Terryn asked, both dismayed and confused by the strange sight.

His light-dragon stood at his right shoulder, long neck arched as it gazed into the valley. *They are under compulsion,* it, said. *They have breathed too much* oblivis, *and they are not their own masters anymore.*

They must belong to Odile. It must be the Witch Queen who commanded them to attack the wall in her efforts to get through to the Eitr Crown. Which meant she must be near. Which meant . . .

Then an image in his shadow vision drew Terryn's attention, and his heart lodged in his throat: A blast of Anathema magic shot through the ranks of monsters had a familiar hue.

He spotted Fendrel almost at once. The Venator Dominus had thrown back his black hood, and his hair streamed wildly behind him as he slashed and blasted with terrible accuracy. Fresh blood streamed from his fingers, an ongoing source of energy for each curse generated.

Terryn's heart went cold. Strange impulses warred within him. First, his training urged him to leap down to Fendrel's assistance, to place himself at his master's right hand and battle beside him. But then . . . this man had ordered Terryn's murder only the night before. Terryn's murder, Gerard's imprisonment, and Ayleth's . . .

"Ayleth," Terryn whispered. Where was she?

Another hood, a red one this time, caught Terryn's eye. He looked more closely and recognized Hollis. He'd freed her from Dunloch earlier that day, and she'd set out in pursuit of Fendrel and Ayleth. If she was here, surely Ayleth must be as well. Had they unbound her hands so she could fight with all her powers and strength? Or had Fendrel insisted on keeping her captive even in the face of such an enemy?

Before Terryn could determine answers, a swarm of monsters descended on Hollis—many long-limbed, unearthly things, moving as one entity, overwhelming her.

"*Hollis!*" Fendrel's voice rang out above the fiendish howls and snarls. A blast of Anathema magic flew at the swarm but scarcely touched the outermost writhing bodies. Three fell away, but more leaped into the place of their fallen brethren.

"*To me, Nisirdi,*" Terryn growled and sprang down the steep incline of the waterfall, leaping from stone to stone while pulling up his shade's power and drawing the heat and light into his palms. A grim smile of satisfaction turned up the corners of his mouth. He was getting better at this, more confident. "*Now!*" he cried and opened his hands.

Two beams of light blasted into the snarl of monsters swarming on top of Hollis. The blast was so great, their mortal bodies disintegrated into dust, but no spirits rose from them—the host body and controlling mind was elsewhere, untouched.

It didn't matter. Hollis lay visible now, limp and bloody on the ground. Terryn ran toward her, but someone got there before him, falling to his knees at her side and lifting her in his arms. Her head rolled against his arm, her long hair loose and matted with blood.

Fendrel buried his face in the top of her head, but pulled back again almost at once, his eyes huge, searching for the source of that light blast. He met Terryn's gaze through the running throngs of shade-taken.

Terryn stopped, his heart sinking to his gut as he looked into his master's eyes. He took a step back.

In that exact moment, he felt something. Something he could hardly describe. It was almost as though a hand gripped the side of his face, urging him to turn his head and look up, away from the battle, to the cliff's edge above. To the place where the land rose highest of all, fifty feet above the valley. Yielding to the impulse, he turned.

He saw Ayleth.

Even without access to her shadow senses, Ayleth felt the explosions of magic. She saw spurts of fire and water, storms of dirt and stone, all the signs of Elemental shades. She saw monsters of hideous proportions, twisted and warped things, both animal and human, and other beings somewhere in between. The songs of Lures screamed through the bloody chaos. The roars of Ferals ripped at the heart. The stench of blood filled her nostrils as Anathema curses flew. And her vision danced with the tangle of bodies and spirits thrashing in the violence of combat.

Worst of all was the vast snarl of vines surrounding the city, now towering higher even than the cliff on which Ayleth stood.

This was why the Witchwood had seemed so strangely still today, why the vines that had been so prevalent during her first journey beyond the Great Barrier were nearly absent. The Witchwood's power was concentrated here in the crown's last defense against the queen who would be its mistress.

A flash of red caught Ayleth's eye—it was a Red Hood in the midst of that nightmarish mass, grappling with monsters. She recognized that square, strong frame. "Kephan," she whispered, breathless. What was he doing down there?

Another flash of red, and this time she identified Hollis. Then another venator whose name she did not know. They fought bravely. Defending the wall? But why?

Did the Witchwood require the help of a handful of Evanderians? But when she returned her attention to the wall of vines, she spied a thin place. The combined force of all those monsters and all that magic might, just *might* be enough to break through the Witchwood's defenses.

Then a swarm of monsters driven by a single mind and purpose descended upon Hollis. Ayleth gasped as she watched her former mistress disappear beneath blackened limbs and chittering jaws.

"No." The word slipped from her lips, too breathless for a scream. "No, Hollis!" Her body jerked with an impulse to dive over the cliff's edge, to throw herself into the fight below. She took a step.

Odile's hand clasped her arm. Startled, Ayleth turned. Black eyes, so wide she could see her own face reflected in their centers, gazed at her with solemn entreaty.

"Remember," Odile said, her voice deep, gentle, but tinged with warning. She placed her hands on Ayleth's cheeks, cupping her face, and bent her head closer until their foreheads touched. Ayleth gazed into those dark pools full of memory, full of pain. Full of love deep and dire enough to make a soul tremble. "Remember, Olena,"

Odile said, "they would burn you alive and call it mercy."

Her heart clenched in her breast. With an effort of will, Ayleth pulled her face away and stared back down into the mayhem, into the place where Hollis had been. Flames danced in her head even as she strained to catch a glimpse of a red hood. "Hollis . . ." she whispered.

A blast of coruscating white light.

Ayleth screamed in pain, flinging up both hands to shield her face. Blindness filled her head, burned her eyes—sparks whirled in the darkness behind her lids. All other senses retreated, leaving her in a weird limbo of pain on the edge of that cliff.

Then a single thought broke through the pain—*light.* Brilliant white light.

Terryn?

Blinking hard against the sparks dancing around the edge of her vision, she stared back down into the battle, searching, searching, until . . . there he was. There, amid that storm of horror and death and pain, he stood. Tall, strong, his eyes brilliant with ascendant power, his hands glowing white with light that burned out from his core.

At any moment the monsters would close in on him;

at any moment he would be overwhelmed, consumed, destroyed. Any moment could be the last she ever saw him alive, so she gazed upon him, drinking in the sight, drinking in that image, drinking in those seconds that would have to last her an eternity.

As though he felt her gaze upon him, Terryn looked up. Their eyes met.

She watched horror spread across his features as he saw who stood beside her.

CHAPTER 13

TERRYN'S SOUL SHUDDERED WITH THE SHOCK OF understanding. He stood transfixed as though caught in a spell.

Hollis hadn't told him. She'd said that Ayleth was the only one who could kill Odile, but she had never said why. She'd never explained to him that the spell keeping Odile alive even through the violence of a beheading was connected to her blood.

Blood which Ayleth shared.

Terryn gazed up to that ledge above the battle, up to where that tall, slim girl stood behind an equally tall, slim specter. Ayleth—vicious, fearless Ayleth. The woman who had caught hold of him body and soul, twisting everything he thought he knew about himself into something strange, something frightening, something he couldn't resist even if he wished to.

Ayleth.

Daughter of Shades. Child of Poison.

The mayhem around him seemed to retreat to an echoing distance. The reverberating blasts of magic, the screams of dying bodies and violently liberated souls scarcely touched his senses. His whole world hung in that space stretched out between him and her, his whole life vibrating through the thread of connection suspended between their locked gazes.

Fendrel had warned him that she was dangerous. A witch. Fendrel had told him he was ensorcelled. He'd given up everything. The Order. His service to Gerard. His very life. All for her. All for the witch's girl.

A sudden ferocious smile split Terryn's face.

A shade-taken loomed on his right, a massive Feral

shrieking with rage, magic bursting from its tortured spirit. Without shifting his gaze, Terryn merely raised his left hand and sent a controlled beam straight through the monster. There was no time to worry about the souls streaking through the ether of this world, no time to consider the roaring Haunts gaping wide above them, seeking to swallow every screaming soul. There was no time to consider anything but the certainty of what he must now do.

Terryn ran. Nisirdi followed at his heels, wings outspread, and the shade-taken horde, observing that massive and ascendant light-dragon's approach, scattered before him, throwing themselves out of his way. Ayleth watched him come, her eyes growing wider and wider with every step he took. Her wrists were still wrapped in iron shackles, and her face was an unreadable blend of emotions, none of which he could name. But she was there. Alive. Standing above him.

"*Nisirdi!*" he shouted to his shade. The light-dragon instantly responded with magic power channeled outward from Terryn's heart into his right arm, which he raised, pointing his fist to that cliff above. Pointing at that tall, slender figure who watched his approach with night-black eyes.

"*Now!*"

Terryn opened his fist, and a bolt of light shot out from his core. It flew straight, true, and instantaneous, blasting a hole through her heart and bursting out the other side.

Ayleth stared at the gaping hole—the blackened skin, the smoldering ash, the empty cavern where flesh and blood and bone ought to be. Her eyes were so dazzled by the flash of light that she thought she must not be seeing things correctly, thought this must be an illusion, a nightmare.

Odile's chin dropped; she stared down at that horrible wound in her breast. Then, slowly, she lifted her eyes, locking her gaze with Ayleth's. It was too much to bear. She had to break that connection, had to recover her own sense of autonomy. Ayleth blinked, severing that gaze.

And in the instant that her eyes were closed, she saw images of Odile's life. All those images, the memories she herself had just lived in that timeless dream state. She saw the trembling bride gazing up at the red-hooded figures on horseback. She saw the weeping mother kneeling in a bed of ash. She saw the magnificent monster standing in the ruin of the great council chamber of Agla, surrounded by death and destruction, the *eitr* crown shining on her head.

She saw her grandmother.

Her eyes opened, and she faced Odile again. Faced that expression of twisted, stunned agony. Ayleth lifted her shackled hands, wanting to reach for her, wanting to take Odile in her arms. Her lips started to form a name—a plea, a prayer perhaps—but her voice faltered on her lips.

Then, from deep in her gut, she sensed the regenerating power of the *Cravan Druch*. The discordant horror of spell threads weaving through reality, playing against all the laws of nature and matter and time. *Oblivis* whirled, churning and pulsing with magic. The still-smoldering hole in Odile's breast began to repair itself.

"Ayleth!"

The voice reached her through the drumming of her

heartbeat in her ears. Dully, she turned, looked down the cliff . . . and saw him. Terryn. Running toward her. Enraged monsters screamed and surrounded him yet shied away from the pulsing power still gleaming in his hands after that blast of Arcane light. She looked into his face and saw the storm of conflict warring there.

He knew. He knew who she was. *What* she was.

"Ayleth!" he shouted again. Light flashed from the depths of his throat. "Do it! *Now!*"

Ayleth whirled on her heel and faced Odile.

Somehow, impossibly, the Witch Queen was still on her feet. Her head lolled back, exposing her throat as she stared up into the sky. *Oblivis* coursed through that gaping wound and twined around her hands, her torso, into her eyes and open mouth. Her hair streamed out behind her like a black flag in the living air.

Something moved in the center of that empty space. Bone, growing like a tree limb, sprouting and taking shape. Layers of sinew, muscle, dainty veins, and flesh reknit, pulled together by the magic of the *Cravan Druch*.

Ayleth took a step, lifted her hands. She couldn't hesitate. For this moment and this moment only, Odile was completely vulnerable. Nothing could stop her from fulfilling her purpose, the whole purpose for which she'd been kept alive all these years.

She must kill the last of her kin.

"Ayleth!" Terryn's voice shouted again as though from a great distance, followed by a wordless roar as he threw some shade-taken monster off his back. "Ayleth, please!"

But Odile's voice echoed in her head: *"We need not be alone anymore. Not now that we have found one another."*

Her soul was frozen. She couldn't move, couldn't think.

Her lips formed a single, desperate word: "Goddess."

Before she could add another breath, Odile's head snapped upright. Her eyes flared wide. The hole through her chest, not yet fully repaired, swarmed with black threads of magic and spell song. Her mouth twisted in agony, agony she experienced completely despite her inability to die. Fighting against that pain, she raised one arm, pointed one finger.

The *oblivis* around her hand transformed into a bolt of shooting darkness. It streaked through the air in a flash and lanced straight through Terryn's heart.

Ayleth choked. Her spirit rocked as though she herself had received that blow.

She saw Terryn's body go stiff as stone. His eyes widened just enough that the whites ringed the icy blue irises. Black veins crept across his skin, spreading swiftly as the *oblivis* ate away at his insides.

He collapsed in a lifeless heap.

Ayleth stared down at the whirl of *oblivis* encircling Terryn's fallen body. She scarcely noticed how the shade-taken monsters drew back from him in terror. She scarcely noticed how close to the cliff's edge she had drawn. She felt nothing, not even sorrow, not even surprise. Nothing.

It wasn't true. It couldn't be true. He'd been dead before, hadn't he? Fendrel had ordered him killed, and he'd died, and she'd lost him, only it wasn't true. He'd escaped somehow, just as he must escape this time. Just as he must miraculously rise up, his spirit burning bright inside his mortal flame, his eyes flashing with light.

She tried to reach out with her shadow senses, tried to get some sense of his soul. But Laranta was too deeply suppressed. She couldn't feel anything.

His dark brown skin turned inky black with writhing movement beneath the skin.

He was dead.

Dead.

Her heart stopped beating. But it didn't matter. Nothing mattered now. Nothing except . . .

Ayleth turned to Odile. Dread Odile, the Witch Queen. The Poison. The Enemy.

With a wild shriek she lunged straight for that scarred neck, hands first. It was too late already, and she knew it, but she didn't care. She threw herself senselessly, manically forward, her whole soul fixated on taking that neck between her hands and—

Oblivis rose in a rush and whirled around Odile in a protective wall. Through the flashing motes, Ayleth saw her grandmother's face, pale and tight with pain and rage. She saw those eyes blacken into endless pits of darkness.

"So," she said, her voice reeking with the stench of the Haunts, "you would side with the Evanderians after all. My own blood. My own Olena."

Her right hand moved in a swift, grasping motion. *Oblivis* lashed out, wrapping around Ayleth. Before she could spring back it hardened into stone—a strange, flexible, mobile stone, too hard to resist yet still floating in the air, coiling, living, and binding her arms against her body. Ayleth bit out a wild, wordless scream, struggled, kicked. She gnashed her teeth so hard that blood and spittle flew from her lips.

Odile observed her coldly. The last of her chest wound healed over, the threads of the spell song pulling tight. She moved her right hand again, this time bringing it up in a short, sharp motion of command.

Out of the *oblivis* binding Ayleth's arms grew a branch, rising to the same level as her eyes. A long spike extended from it, the point stretching, stretching. Ayleth tried to pull back, but the oblidite bands held her fast. The spike pressed against her temple, its point drawing blood that ran down her cheek in a stream. The slightest pressure more and it would pierce her skull.

Before her stood Odile, her skin deathly white but for the black wound around her throat. "Never forget, my child," she said, "I would have chosen your life. I would have let you stand beside me to the end of your days. I would have loved you, if only you had let me."

CHAPTER 14

HOLLIS.

Hollis, wake up.

We need you.

I need you.

Hollis!

She stood at a crossroads deep in the labyrinth of her mind. The voice echoed from one of the five corridors before her, but it struck the stone walls, bounced, and bounced again, echoing until she couldn't decide where the sound had originated. She turned slowly, gazing down one shadowy tunnel after another.

Hollis!

Please!

The walls seemed to vibrate with the urgency of that voice. The entire world of her mind shook in response, the ground rumbling beneath her unsteady feet. She reached out for her shade, hoping its powers might help to guide her. But it had retreated deep into one of the other tunnels of her mind, momentarily out of her reach. She was on her own.

She faced one tunnel, then slowly turned all the way around to face the one behind her. She took a step. Then, on impulse, she whirled again and ran down the first corridor, fast enough that she couldn't second-guess her decision. The echoes became louder and louder with every step she took.

Hollis!

Hollis!

Hollis!

Suddenly an opening. Light. She burst through and—

Fendrel's face appeared above her, framed by long

dirty strands of fair hair. She stared up at him, blinking blearily. Was she . . . was she cradled in his arms? The sensation was strangely familiar.

"Hollis?" He was as pale as death, his eyes sunken deep behind dark circles. Until that moment she'd never realized how much he'd aged in the last twenty years. "Hollis, can you hear me?"

She nodded. Her voice emerged in a rough rasp, "Yes. I hear you. I'm all right." She tried to move and winced. One exploratory hand found a gash on the side of her face, bleeding profusely. Her leather armor boasted another slash along her ribcage, but it hadn't cut through to skin and bone. She was battered but not broken. She looked around, blinking harder, trying to make her dizzy eyes focus. She was not on the field of battle where she'd fallen. Fendrel crouched behind a large stone, holding her. He must have carried her here.

How had he even gotten to her? The last thing she remembered was that swarm of monsters piling on top of her. She'd thought she was done for.

The air was tense, weirdly still. Even the motes of *oblivis* floating everywhere seemed to have frozen in place.

"What's going on?" Hollis demanded, looking up at Fendrel again.

He met her gaze, and she suddenly wished she hadn't asked. "Odile," he said.

A shadow fell across Hollis's soul. Gripping Fendrel's arm, she pulled herself up. "Careful," he warned, but she hardly heard him. She peered out from around the stone.

And she saw her—Odile. The Poison. Floating down from the cliff above on a cloud of *oblivis*. She still wore the tatters of her crypt garments, but they seemed to hang from her limbs like royal robes. Her hair, which had burned away twenty years ago, was now restored, thick and dark and glossy as though rubbed with expensive oils, and it wafted behind her like a royal train. Her posture was upright, her hands spread to each side as though offering benediction to the masses. She looked like a queen indeed. Or like a goddess descending from heaven.

Her horde of shade-taken ceased their wild attack on the wall and abased themselves before her, groveling and writhing as she passed by. But Hollis scarcely saw this. Her gaze focused instead on that which came behind Odile—Ayleth, wrapped in bonds of *oblivis*, with a spike pressed to her temple. She floated behind the queen, her feet several inches above the ground, helpless.

Hollis growled and moved to lunge from her hiding place. Fendrel's grip landed on her arm like iron, hauling her back. "Don't be a fool," he snarled in her ear.

Hollis shot him a furious look. What else were they supposed to do? Ayleth was their only chance to kill the witch. They had to free her! But Fendrel's grip was unbreakable.

Odile passed across the narrow valley, pausing briefly over something lying in her path. Looking closer, Hollis realized with a twist in her gut what it was: Terryn. His body lay with limbs outspread, convulsing in death throes. His veins stood out stark and black and thick beneath his skin as *oblivis* poison overcame him, body and soul. Hollis glanced up at Fendrel again. Seeing the expression on his face, she had to turn away quickly.

Odile continued, leading her captive on her leash of *oblivis*. From this angle, Hollis could not see Ayleth's face. Was the girl still alive?

Odile progressed through her adoring throng until she stood before the wall of vines with Ayleth held at her side. Her monsters swarmed in behind her, forming an arch at her back. They gazed at her with devotion, whimpering, salivating, burying their faces in the dirt.

"Oromor!" Odile cried out in a loud voice that rang across the valley. "I have her, Oromor. I have her, and I will end her now unless you let me pass."

The wall shook. The roots of the vines deep underground moved, massive lumps rippling beneath the rotten soil. Tendrils emerged here and there, grabbed several of the shade-taken, and dragged them screaming down into the earth.

Untouched amid the turmoil, Odile lifted one hand. Ayleth screamed. She was alive!

Hollis's body reacted on impulse. She halfway leaped out from behind the stone. Fendrel caught her again and yanked her roughly back. "She'll kill you," he growled. "Then she'll kill the girl. You can't stop her."

Tears fell hot down Hollis's face. She did not try to wipe them away.

"Let me through, Oromor," Odile said again. "All your hope for this world lies with her. The last of Mauval's blood runs in her veins. There are no more. Just her, just me. I'll kill her, and I'll still get through to you eventually. You cannot keep me out forever. Let me in, and I may yet allow the girl to live."

The wall shook wildly as the vines twined tighter, constricting like snakes. Hollis felt the waves of wrath and frustration emanating from that vast mind, a mind she dared not directly touch again. She gripped the stone she crouched behind so hard that her fingers bled.

Then, abruptly, the vines pulled back. An opening appeared, small at first, but slowly lengthening until it was equal to Odile's height.

"Wider, Oromor," Odile said.

The opening widened at her command.

It was a trap. It had to be. Surely the moment she got too near, the vines would catch and crush her as they had her many minions. It could not kill her, but perhaps it could slow her long enough that they might get Ayleth free, and . . .

"Play me false, and the girl dies," Odile said. She took hold of Ayleth's shoulder and stepped forward with the confidence of a queen, dragging the girl in her bindings along with her. Hollis saw the spike at Ayleth's temple spinning slowly, and blood flowed in a steady trickle. They passed through the opening, and the vines wound shut behind them.

Hollis leaped up and ran. She paid no heed to the shade-taken, which slinked away to the edges of the valley, watching wide-eyed and silent now that their compulsion had ended. She threw herself at the wall, at that place where the opening had appeared only moments ago. But there was nothing. Not even the barest crack between the woven vines. And they were as hard as rock, impervious to her pounding hands, to her stabbing iron spike. Resistant to her tears and pleading.

Ayleth was gone. Dead. Or as good as dead. And Odile would have the crown. It was only a matter of time, and not much time at that.

With a despairing sob, Hollis turned away from the wall and gazed out across the valley, across all those slaughtered creatures, their souls long since escaped or swallowed up by the hungry Haunts. The Haunts themselves had closed again, but Hollis felt a thinness in the world, as though the horrors of that realm were just waiting to break through the fragile veil and devour them all.

At the edges of her vision, she saw red hoods move. Three of them . . . her other three companions, miraculously still alive. Kephan wore a new gash across his brow, and the venatrix's left arm hung limp, a bone protruding where it shouldn't. The bearded venator moved to assist his hunt sister. Hollis looked away, searching for Fendrel.

She gasped.

Fendrel knelt over Terryn's body. The young venator had ceased convulsing and lay as though dead. But Fendrel had already opened the boy's shirt and was stripped to the waist himself. She saw him put a knife to his scarred chest and press its point at the peak of his collarbone.

"Fendrel!" she cried. He paused to look up at her, and she raced to his side, falling to her knees beside Terryn's body. "What are you doing?" she demanded, reaching to take the knife from him.

He turned, blocking her hand with his shoulder. "I'm going to save the boy."

She shook her head. "You can't. You . . . you have

nothing to pass the curse into."

"That doesn't matter now," Fendrel said. He met Hollis's gaze, his expression stern. "It doesn't matter, Hollis. And I need your help."

"Fendrel . . ." She shook her head, hiding behind her curtain of hair for the space of a breath. Then she looked up again, steeling her face. "You bound your soul to your shade. If you die . . ."

"I am damned," he finished for her. "Whether I die today, tomorrow, next year . . . I am damned." He swallowed hard. His voice was steady, his features hard as stone, but she saw the fear in his eyes. "I will save Terryn before I go."

She shook her head again, tears streaming fast.

"He's so far gone," Fendrel continued. "This blast . . . it was too much, and he has minutes at most, possibly much less. I've got to find him in his mind. I've got to make him hold on while I purge the *oblivis*. Will you help me? Will you bridge our minds?"

She couldn't answer. She didn't know what to say. Her stomach heaved as if with sickness, but it was her heart that hurt.

With a choking sob, she reached out, pressed her hand to his forehead, and closed her eyes, stepping into the labyrinth world of her mind and facing the long dark tunnels.

"*Come to me!*" she cried.

Her shade responded in a whir of a hundred wings.

Terryn fled across the plains of his mind, wading through the tall grasses. The last time he was here, the grass was green and lush, full of vibrant new life. Now it was dry, dead. Waiting for a single spark to set it all ablaze.

Darkness rolled in above him like a thunderhead. But this was no lightning storm brewing. This was *oblivis*, pure *oblivis* shot straight to his soul. It would tear him apart.

He knew what to do. Panting hard, he drove himself harder, forcing his legs to take longer and longer strides as he leapt through the dead rustling grass. Nisirdi. Nisirdi had successfully burned out the *oblivis* he'd breathed earlier that day, when the Phantomwitch tried to leave him in the Haunts. Surely his shade could manage the feat again. He just had to find his light-dragon.

The ground beneath his feet groaned, shifted. Began to tear. The landscape broke in hairline cracks which grew, widening by the second. Darkness seemed to pour up from the deeps like a flood of shadows sweeping over the plains.

Terryn skidded to a stop as a crack opened right in front of him. He cursed, turned, and bolted another way. But the ground broke again, and he was only just nimble enough to leap, flying across the empty drop. He hit the far side, legs dangling, arms scrambling, and managed to pull his body up. He got to his feet, drew breath, and took three steps.

The ground gave way beneath him, and he fell.

Down, down into darkness deep and suffocating.

"*Nisirdi!*" he cried. But no answer came.

He landed hard. Had he been in his mortal body, he would have broken every bone. As it was, his mind struggled to comprehend that he wasn't broken, that this body was a mere projection and therefore not limited to mortal failings. He lay for some while with pain shooting through every limb and bursting in his brain. But eventually the pain subsided and there was only darkness.

Then . . . light. Faint white light, far away but clear.

Terryn gathered his arms beneath him, pushed up onto his hands and knees, and managed to get to his feet. He seemed to be in a tunnel. A vague impression of rock surrounded him and arched over his head. There was nothing down here except that distant glow, and he started toward it. It must be Nisirdi. It *must* be. And if he could find his light-dragon, surely he could still be saved.

"*Terryn! Terryn!*"

He stopped. That was Gerard's voice calling from just behind him, a little to his right. The urge to turn, to look, was nearly overwhelming.

But no. He mustn't turn. He knew what this was—a lure to keep him from achieving his goal. Gerard was not here, not really. This was his own mind suffering under poison. He could not help Gerard; he could not help anyone unless he could get free.

Steeling his will, Terryn continued. Gerard called after him, his voice strained and sad. "*Terryn! Terryn, help me!*"

Each step away from that voice was an agony. But he must endure it if there was to be any hope of salvation.

Then a new voice called to him. A woman's voice,

deep and low. *"Terryn. Terryn, help me. Please."*

Ayleth.

She sounded as if she were just behind him, not even an arm's length away. He could turn around, reach out, and take her in his arms. He could love her. Even if she was nothing more than a projection, what did that matter? Perhaps the real Ayleth was lost to him forever. Perhaps she was not who he thought she was. But here in his mind, she could be exactly what he wanted, exactly what he needed.

The temptation was there, and she was so close . . . but it was only a lie. A lie born of the *oblivis* coursing through his blood, through his spirit. He must reach that light!

Terryn moved faster, leaving her voice echoing desperately behind him. *"Terryn! Please!"*

The light intensified. He was getting closer now. He'd reach his shade soon, and then he'd be free. He just had to push a little harder, to not let the darkness persuade him, not let the *oblivis* influence him. He just had to—

"Terryn."

He stopped short.

A figure stood at his right hand, just within his

peripheral vision. He would have to turn his head only a fraction to see that face clearly. That well-known face. Those iron-gray eyes under that stern brow.

"Terryn, I'm here. I can help you. Don't fight me, boy. Look at me. Look at me!"

It was another trick. Another temptation. He dared not be swayed from his goal.

The white light at the end of the tunnel flickered, faded.

"Terryn, don't be a fool. You know me. You know I can save you. Come to me now. Give me your hand. I can take this from you—"

Terryn ran. He poured all his strength into putting space between him and that voice he'd been brought up all his life to obey. But he knew better now. Fendrel was a liar! He had betrayed Terryn, betrayed Gerard, betrayed all of Perrinion. Even if he was real and not some projection of the *oblivis* trying to overcome his mind, Terryn knew better than to believe him.

So he ran and ran, his gaze fixed upon that shining light.

Suddenly the tunnel opened into a broad cavern.

Terryn skidded to a halt, his arms wheeling as he strove to catch his balance. His feet danced on the edge of a short drop. And below him, not three lengths down . . .

He caught his breath. His eyes widened with horror.

Down below him was Nisirdi, caught in a pit of black and burning tar. The once-magnificent white wings strove to beat free, but oozing black liquid weighted them down on either side, dragging the light-dragon deeper and deeper. Its long, elegant neck stretched, struggling to keep its head above the boiling surface. Nisirdi gazed up at Terryn with huge globe eyes full of sorrow, full of fear.

I'm so sorry, it said as the blackness pulled it deeper still.

CHAPTER 15

TERRYN . . .

It was her fault.

If she'd acted at once she could have saved him. She could have saved all of them. Odile could not have fought her off, not then, not with that massive hole through her chest, not while she waited for the *Cravan Druch* to do its work. She could have ended it all there and then, even without Laranta's help.

But she'd hesitated. Haunts damn her, she'd hesitated

at the moment of crisis like a rabbit freezing in the flash of the hunter's torch.

And now Terryn . . .

Terryn . . .

Her mind refused to complete the thought. For the moment it refused to function at all. Forces beyond her control carried her along in a current of death and destruction she would never escape. And Odile walked beside her.

Vines crawled along the ground behind them and on either side. Creeping like so many subtle snakes, they kept pace with Odile as she progressed along the Queen's Highway, holding tight to Ayleth with many strands of hardened *oblivis*, the oblidite spike still pressed to her temple. Slowly Ayleth's vision cleared, and she began to notice the world around her. She'd walked this road before, in her dreams. It was familiar to her, but its very familiarity made it that much more surreal.

The reality of the destruction was harsher than any dream could accurately depict. In dreams she hadn't felt the weight of the fallen stones around her, the pressure as they sank into the sucking earth. In dreams she'd detected only the faintest trace of rot and decay and broken magic, not the pungent and pervasive stench that now assaulted her nostrils. She hadn't felt the haunting echoes that whispered up and down the vacant streets and along the empty canals, whispering of lives long since gone, of glories long since brought to ruin. It was much worse than Ayleth would have expected after a mere twenty years of neglect. The remains of Dulimurian looked as though they had festered here a century or more.

But despite the ruin, despite the rot, despite the brokenness surrounding her, assailing her senses, Odile strode along with quick steps. This was her city, her world, carved out by the blood she'd spilled during two centuries of domination—the blood of others as well as her own. If seeing it brought so low distressed her, she showed no sign. As she proceeded with all the solemn confidence of a ruling queen, clouds of *oblivis* wafted in her wake.

Vines emerged from the gaping windows of fallen structures, their tendril fingers writhing in the air as though only just keeping themselves from lashing out. Ayleth sensed the lust pulsing through them to take hold of Odile, to tear her apart. The same desire echoed in her own howling soul.

But she could do nothing. Even if she still had access to Laranta's powers, she wouldn't stand a chance against Odile and the Elemental she carried. And without shade magic to aid her, she was entirely helpless.

They reached a place where the road broke and the ground split in a huge chasm. Odile strode up to the edge so swiftly that Ayleth thought for a moment she wouldn't even pause, would go right over and plunge into the darkness below, dragging Ayleth with her. But just at the last instant she stopped. Ayleth, suspended in the *oblivis,* hovered partway over the drop, staring down into indescribable depths.

Odile snarled softly, a wordless curse, and gazed across to where the Queen's Highway resumed on the other side of the chasm. Some massive shift in the world had shoved this part of the road up to form an outcropping that jutted some fifty feet overhead.

Ayleth pulled her gaze from the drop to study Odile's expression, fully expecting the Witch Queen to summon more *oblivis* and build a bridge for herself. Or perhaps simply to gather it in a thick enough cloud to carry her and Ayleth up and across.

But no. On second glance, Odile was terribly pale. Though she held her body straight and tall, she could not fully disguise the tremor running up and down her spine. That blast from Terryn, though unable to kill her, had drained her strength. The *Cravan Druch* song spell sustained her, held her together, but it took nearly all the shade magic she controlled just to stay upright while simultaneously maintaining Ayleth's bindings. For the moment at least, she lacked the power to cross the ravine.

Vines crawling in and out of the buildings and along the edges of the road hissed as their twining bodies rubbed against one another. It sounded like laughter. Like victory.

Odile lifted her hands. Ayleth rose higher in the air, spinning slowly in the bindings of *oblivis*. She wanted to kick, wanted to scream, wanted to thrash and struggle and make it as difficult as possible for Odile to maintain her grasp on her. But the pressure of the spike in her temple increased, and her neck muscles ached with the effort to hold her head perfectly still.

"Do you see her, Oromor?" Odile said. Her voice was smooth as silk and terribly soft. "Do you see her, the last of Mauval's bloodline? The last hope you have in this world? I will kill her."

The spike rotated. Ayleth screamed. She tried to swallow it, but the sound ripped from her throat beyond her ability to control. The vines shrieked in response, shivered, and pulled away from the edges of the road, vanishing from view into the empty structures.

Ayleth, blinking through the haze of terror and pain storming in her head, saw movement in the empty space above the chasm. A twining, thickening gleam of magic and darkness. The *oblivis* in the air hardened into long coils extending from one side of the chasm to the other. The coils twined together, then solidified into hardened oblidite, creating a bridge that looked both plantlike and stone at once. It was a steep incline leading up to that crest fifty feet above.

Odile let out a long, satisfied breath and stepped forward swiftly. She waved one beckoning hand, drawing the *oblivis* bindings with her so that Ayleth floated through the air in her wake. Ayleth couldn't believe she trusted the bridge to hold. She would have expected the Witchwood to play them false, to wait until they were over the center of the chasm and then let the bridge disintegrate back into its raw *oblivis* form.

But the bridge held. They reached the solid ground high on the far side. With the pressure of the oblidite spike still sharp against her temple, Ayleth saw a straight, clear stretch through the ruins of the city, leading to the tiered steps beneath Odile's broken idol. Vines swarmed on either side of the road, climbing and tearing and breaking the blocks of oblidite in undisguised fits of frustration. Huge chunks of faceted stone crashed to the ground, shaking the world.

Odile continued, her stride purposeful, resolute, and light as a dancer's step. High above, the broken idol's upraised hand glowed with blue light. The Presence was there, looking down on them, sending out its thousands of questing, eager fingers.

Why would such a being desire a human host? Wasn't the Witchwood itself a far superior, more powerful, more lethal host than a human body could ever hope to be? But there was something so desperate, so yearning in the whispering vines around them. A longing focused on Ayleth herself, she realized with a shudder of horror. As though she—or at the least the blood flowing in her veins—were the last great hope for all salvation.

"They were incarnate once, you know," Odile spoke suddenly. Ayleth couldn't move save to flick her eyes to one side. She could just discern the Witch Queen's stern profile, her black eyes focused on the idol, on the blue glow cupped in its hand. Whether she had spoken for Ayleth's benefit or simply mused aloud, Ayleth couldn't guess. "The shades," she continued in that same smooth, gentle voice. "The *Ildrir.*"

The word spoken with a mortal tongue mingled with a shadow voice and struck Ayleth's ear in a strange clash of sound and meaning. Her soul rang with a complexity of time and non-time, of space and non-space, of contradict-tions and ideas and bursts of inexplicable light that her brain couldn't quite contain.

"They wore incarnate forms not unlike our own," Odile said. "But over time . . . time greater than anything you or I can imagine . . . they ascended. They expanded their minds, their souls. Their songs. In order to channel the music they composed, they built greater instruments, such as the Songstones of Morlorn and others. With the aid of those instruments, they expanded further still."

The one black eye Ayleth could see from her angle was wide, white-ringed. Manic. As though Odile gazed upon pure madness and knew that if she did not blink soon, she would be lost. At the last possible instant, she closed her eyes and turned her head to one side.

"I have seen much," she said, her voice still soft, low, melodious. "Through the memory of the shade I carry, I have explored into the depths and witnessed things I cannot describe. There is much yet that I do not know, much more I will never know."

She opened her eyes again, concentrating on the road before them, her face set like stone. Not once did she glance Ayleth's way, though she maintained a careful grip on her bindings. "What I do know is this: There came a time when the shades—the *Ildrir*—stepped beyond their incarnate bodies and pursued a new existence of pure, fleshless spirit. They believed they were gods. They thought they might remake the worlds after their own design. They thought . . . they believed . . . and when it was too late . . . only then did they realize what they had lost . . ."

Her voice trailed away to nothing. Ayleth couldn't imagine where such a speech could go from there. Even as the spike at her temple drew beads of blood with every beat of her heart, her mind tried to grapple with the words the Witch Queen had spoken. Was Odile actually saying that the shades had not always been shades? And that they longed to return to the incarnate forms they once wore, to return to the physical worlds they once inhabited?

Was this why the Presence waited for them above, watching with such eagerness as they approached? Despite the greatness of the Witchwood, the mighty host it had created for itself through the empowerment of the *Atacara,* did it still hunger to reclaim a form closer to that which it had once enjoyed in eons lost to memory?

If so, Ayleth was still alive only because the Presence wanted her, with her du Mauvalis blood still warm and flowing in her veins. Odile knew that if she killed Ayleth now, the Witchwood would never let her anywhere near the *eitr* crown. It may not be able to kill her, but, judging by the amount of power Ayleth sensed churning through the vines around them, it could tear her apart. Over and over again. For the rest of her existence.

Yet Odile walked into that viper's nest with confidence because she had Ayleth in her grasp. Because she had that spike aimed at her brain.

They reached the stairs leading up to the idol's monolith base, so steep that Ayleth would have been forced to use her hands as well as her feet to climb them were she moving of her own volition. But Odile's *oblivis* simply lifted and carried her so that her feet scarcely touched the treads, while Odile herself floated along at her side, hands outstretched, *oblivis* twining through her fingers. Her gaze remained fixed on the top of the stair.

The idol's hand stretched directly over their heads, its shadow blacker than night yet edged with blue light falling in streams of magic like a silent waterfall. The *eitr* was awake, alive. Aware.

"You lied to me," Ayleth said suddenly. It was the first she'd tried to speak since watching Terryn's death. Her voice was hoarse, almost unrecognizable even to her own ears.

Odile's gaze remained fixed on her goal above.

"This was your intention all along," Ayleth persisted. "To use me. Just like the rest of them did. I am your tool to get back your crown. Nothing more."

Odile's face was so perfectly still, she seemed not to have heard.

"Was any of it real? All those visions you showed me—those moments of your life? Was it nothing but more manipulation? To make me see myself in you?" She couldn't shake her head. The spike was too close. Blood rolled down her cheek and neck. Her lips quivered and her voice broke. "Olena. That isn't my name, is it? It's all just a story."

No flicker of remorse touched Odile's face. No pause, no momentary lapse in concentration. She was as hard as the oblidite over which she floated.

"No past," Ayleth whispered. "No future."

Her blood boiled. With rage. With bloodlust.

This was all she could ever be. All she was ever meant to be. By the Goddess's design or the will of others, this was the truth of her existence. A tool. An instrument of destruction. A weapon.

And the only person who had seen anything more in her . . . the only one who had looked her in the eye and seen who she was, not what she could be . . . he was gone.

Ayleth set her teeth, breathing sharply in and out through flaring nostrils. "Only the hunt," she growled.

They reached the summit of the stairs at last and stepped onto the wide platform base. It was just as black and gleaming as it had been in Ayleth's dreams. The Witchwood had done nothing to mar its smooth perfection. But the idol was a different story. Broken off partway up its legs, it ought to have fallen long ago, crushing the city streets below. The whole structure tilted at a dangerous angle.

Yet somehow it stood, defying all the laws of nature. Vines twined up its smooth-carved limbs, covering the nakedness of that womanly form. The feet, calves, and shins had crumbled away, but through the rubble, through the tangle of vines, Ayleth spied a gaping hole in the knee, revealing the stairway inside.

Odile charged forward, pushing Ayleth ahead in her *oblivis* bindings. She paused at the opening to the staircase only long enough to reach out one hand and grasp the ragged edges of the makeshift doorway. The opening widened, and Ayleth watched in disbelief as the stairs solidified, leading in a seemingly endless spiral up into the idol's torso. Odile glanced Ayleth's way and made another short motion with her hand. Ayleth's feet sank to the ground. Her arms were still bound, and the spike continued to hover at her head.

"Climb," Odile commanded.

Ayleth breathed out through clenched teeth. But what choice did she have? She couldn't force Odile to kill her. Not now. Not yet. Odile still needed her alive. By refusing to climb, she would simply lose what little liberty she had. At least now she was on her own two feet.

She began the climb up that long spiral. Round and round, only two steps ahead of her captor. The walls sometimes closed in too fast, but at a touch from Odile, they expanded again. Ayleth's side ached, her broken ribs protesting with every breath she took, and her wounded leg throbbed. Yet she pressed on until she thought for certain she wouldn't be able to make one more turn . . . and the stair abruptly came to an end.

Ayleth stepped out onto the statue's shoulder, high above the world. The landscape swept out before her vision on all sides—the concentric rings of Dulimurian's streets were like ripples spreading from the center at the idol's base. The vast expanse of the Witchwood surrounded the city ruins like an ocean of darkness, but from this height Ayleth could see beyond it to the open country of Wodechran Borough. She half convinced herself that she saw Dunloch's four white towers gleaming.

The sun was setting heavy and red in the distance. As though stretching out to grab that burning orb, the arm of the idol extended before her, a bridge to nothing. Nothing but the blue light it held cupped in the palm of its hand.

Was that a voice she heard whispering on the edge of her suppressed shadow senses? A song, a pleading . . . a promise . . .

The spike at her temple turned, rotating to the left just slightly. Ayleth choked on a breath. "Walk," Odile said.

Ayleth stepped out onto that extended arm. Within three paces, her stomach jolted and her core quaked with such dread that she almost froze in place. The arm was broad enough, even over the curving slope of the bicep. She didn't have any real fear of falling. But for the first time in her life, Ayleth felt the true dread of a fall. She tried to shake it off. She'd walked heights as great as this in her dreams before.

But in dreams, no matter how convincing, the dreamer always knows somewhere in the back of her mind that it isn't *real.*

This was real. Very real. Painfully real.

Ayleth inched out across the bridge, one step following the next. There was no wind, nothing to stir her hair, nothing to cool her flushed cheeks. The world seemed to have sucked in its breath, preparing for a huge gust. She felt the gaping void below her. Only a single misstep to the right or to the left . . . only one fractional movement from the spike at her temple . . . and she would fall into an eternity of torment.

She took a step—and saw Hollis's face before her mind's eye. Hollis, perched on a low stool beside the hearth, gazing down at the child seated at her knee, teaching her how to clean and oil her scorpiona, showing her how to repair a broken string.

She took another step—and saw Gerard. Gerard as she had first met him, kneeling in the ruins of the old abbey beside the broken body of a shade-taken, holding the creature by the hand and singing the prayer songs over its remains. Gerard, gentle and brave. The Golden Prince as she'd always dreamed he would be.

She took another step. This time the pale face of Lady Cerine presented itself to her view. Cerine, with her close-cropped hair, standing over Ayleth with the broken remains of a chamber pot in her hands, her eyes wide with terror and courage. Gerard's bride, a true queen in the making.

Another step. Now it was a small, pinch-faced waif who appeared before her. Little Nilly du Bucheron, popping up from where she had fallen among tall ferns to stare at Ayleth with such fear in her little face. Fear . . . and highly ascendant Seer magic, which gleamed in her innocent inborn eyes.

Another step. She saw Kephan as he sat astride his horse, his gaze turned down the western road. "We are not what we think we are," he said, his voice a distant echo in her memory. "In the end, I fear we may discover that we were the true monsters all along."

Another step. Another. And another.

And now, she saw the face she had been trying so hard not to see. She saw him standing at the base of the staircase in Dunloch, his eyes upturned to her. A flash of surprise shot across his features . . . and another expression, more fleeting still. An expression he swiftly masked, only now . . .

Too late! Too late! She'd failed Terryn. She'd failed Gerard and his bride. She'd failed little Nilly and Hollis and Kephan. All of them.

Her feet stepped from a smooth forearm onto a delicately formed wrist. She climbed the gentle rise to the heel of the hand and gazed down the slope into the waiting palm where, for the first time, she saw the *eitr* crown. Not as a dream, not as a memory, not as a projection. The real crown—brilliant and pulsing with light. A living thing.

The Presence hovered like darkness within its central ring. Ayleth didn't need ascendant shadow senses to feel it, to feel longing arms reach out to embrace her. If

Odile's restraints hadn't bound her fast, she would have been tempted to lunge forward and take up that circlet, take up that power. No matter what doom it intended for her, it might also give her strength enough to stop Odile. To undo even one of her own failures.

Odile glided to her side. Ayleth felt the throb of her spirit, so eager, so desperate. "At last," she whispered, her voice shuddering with passion. She took a step ahead of Ayleth.

In that moment, a figure peeled away from the pillar thumb of the statue and took three swift strides. A sword flashed in the dying sunlight as the blade swung back.

Odile turned.

Before she could cry out, before she could lift a finger in her own defense, a blade of pure oblidite cut through her neck. Her head fell from her shoulders and rolled across the palm of the idol's hand.

CHAPTER 16

WITH A GASP, HOLLIS PULLED HER HAND FROM Fendrel's forehead and flung it out to catch herself before she sprawled headlong. Fendrel uttered a vicious curse and sagged over Terryn's body, blood dripping from his wounds. Cuts marked Terryn's torso in the same ugly pattern as Fendrel's, and Hollis's shadow-vision could see the threads of Anathema magic connecting them, blood to blood, and the pulse of *oblivis* flowing from Terryn's body into Fendrel's.

But the young venator didn't look improved. The level of poison infesting both his mortal frame and his spirit substance was so great . . .

At the edges of her vision, Hollis saw Kephan and the other two Evanderians standing protectively close by, facing toward the shade-taken creatures. But the shade-taken hung back, watching the wall, watching the city, watching for some sign of their queen.

The ground shook, and a rumble rolled in from the distance as though some huge structure had fallen on the far side of the wall. The Evanderians staggered to keep their feet, and Hollis nearly fell on her face again. She braced herself on one elbow, and Fendrel bowed over Terryn's body. The branching veins beneath his skin had darkened to black, thickened like ropes. He had already taken in so much poison. But it wasn't nearly enough.

"Fendrel," Hollis said, pushing herself back onto her knees. She tried to catch his eye. "Fendrel, you've got to stop. You've got to—"

"No!" Fendrel's snarl flashed up at her, sharp and deadly. "I found him; I reached him. He's still in there. I've got to make him hold on. I can still do this."

Hollis shook her head. Her ascendant shade danced in the forefront of her brain, and she felt how little control she had over it without renewing the binding song spells. It could tear free of all remaining suppressions in an instant, and her soul would be compromised. "It's too dangerous," she whispered.

His expression twisted with extreme pain and equally intense ferocity. "Please, Hollis." Sweat streamed down his face, blood streamed down his body, and she knew he couldn't take in much more of the poison before he would be beyond all recovery.

Every instinct rebelled. Every instinct told her to tackle him, to break the spell threads, to break that connection. To save Fendrel's life. But she'd tried to save him before, and he wouldn't be saved. If she knew one thing for absolute certain in this world, it was that when Fendrel du Glaive set his mind on a course of action, no one and nothing could stop him. She might as well try to turn back the tide.

"Please," Fendrel begged. "If I can just—"

She raised her arm and pressed her hand to his forehead once more. Her shade power flared bright in their minds.

The stench of boiling tar blistered his senses. Sweat poured down his face as Terryn cast his gaze wildly around the cavern, searching for something, anything he might use to help Nisirdi. But there was nothing. Only those hard, close walls of stone running with rivulets of black tar.

Nisirdi's wings made thick-sounding slaps as they struggled to break the tar's grip. It wasn't truly tar. Terryn knew well enough that what he saw imprisoning and swallowing his shade was the *oblivis* poison in his soul— the bolt Odile shot straight into him was far more concentrated and deadly than the gulp of *oblivis* he'd breathed earlier that day. The black ooze splashed up the sides of the pit, spattering his boots with sizzling droplets. More tar rolled in thicker globules down the walls on either side and dripped in thick ribbons from the low ceiling. The light-dragon sank lower, its long neck extended as far as it could reach.

"*Fight it, Nisirdi,*" Terryn begged. "*Shine brighter and burn it away. I know you have the power in you!"*

But Nisirdi shook its head, then cried out, *No, Terryn! Do not try to reach me.*

Terryn paused in midstep. He'd moved impulsively, a foolish, insane idea driving him to venture in, wade out to his shade, and physically pull it from the tar's grasp. But that was madness. Nisirdi's warning voice snapped him back to reality, at least for the moment.

You must flee this place, the light-dragon urged as it sank lower still. Its mighty wings were now completely overwhelmed. Only the upward curves still arched above the boiling surface, and a film of clinging tar obscured their glow. Splashes of darkness covered most of the dragon's shining neck. The light gleamed through only in patches, flickering dangerously like a torch sputtering in rain. *You must run. Now.*

"Where can I run?" Terryn shook his head. He collapsed to his knees on the edge of the pit. *"There is nowhere safe. Not anymore. Not without you."*

For the first time since Odile's blast struck him, he understood: He was going to die. No more last-minute escapes. No more miraculous recoveries. The tricks of his life were played out, and now there was only the end.

He shook his head ruefully. As a child, as a youth, he never would have believed such a fate lay before him—to be struck down in battle by Dread Odile herself. Memories of those final moments played before his mind. His heart twisted, and he pressed a hand to his breast. Had he understood what took place? Had there been some mistake in his perception?

Had Ayleth truly betrayed him?

That was the most painful thought of all, even here in this stinking, scorching darkness, as he watched his shade's power fade, watched his own life being swallowed up—the idea that Ayleth had sided at last with the Witch Queen. Even shackled in iron as she was, she could have ended Odile's life when the witch stood there with a smoking hole right through her chest. But Ayleth had hesitated.

Was it hesitation? Or was it a choice?

Terryn bowed his head. Fendrel had been right all along. He'd let his emotions play him for a fool. Ayleth was his one great weakness. His ultimate undoing.

Nisirdi's globe eyes blinked up at him. The light-dragon sank to its jaw. The only light remaining in the cavern came from those glowing eyes. When the tar swallowed those as well, final darkness would claim Terryn's mindscape. And then . . . death.

"*I'm sorry, Nisirdi,*" he said, his voice low and heavy. "*I'm sorry it has come to this. I'm sorry we did not have more time to achieve your purpose in this world.*"

A strange, bell-like sound filled the room, rich and light . . . and bizarre in such a horrific setting. It took Terryn several breaths to realize that it was the sound of laughter.

What is time? Nisirdi sang in its strange language. The sound was not so beautiful as it had once been, half drowned now by the tar rolling down from the walls. But it was still pure. *Time has no power, mortal man. A mere passing of hours, of years, of centuries.*

The light-dragon made a strange, gulping gasp as tar poured into its mouth. With a last effort, it pushed its head higher and, for a moment, its eyes flared bright enough to fill the chamber with dancing, iridescent beams. *I am glad my name is known by you, Terryn du Balafre. I am glad that we—*

With a last thick-sounding gulp, the *oblivis* sucked the light-dragon down. The air steamed and sizzled and reeked of burnt tar. For a last moment, Terryn's desperate eyes saw the outline of Nisirdi's head shining through a film of black ooze. Then the darkness was complete. There was only the stench, the heat, the shadows pressing in.

Terryn knelt on the brink of the pit, his head bowed. He knew he was still alive. He could feel his physical body suffering but still clinging to life. It would be only a few more moments now. Without Nisirdi's light shining inside him, fighting off the *oblivis,* he would not last much longer.

The tar bubbled up in the pit, ran down from the walls, and swept toward him, soon to overwhelm him, to boil his spirit alive. He felt it touch the edges of his soul. Lifting his head, he stared up into utter blackness through which he could catch no glimpse of heaven. He raised his hands to the level of his face, open in either pleading or acceptance—he couldn't say which.

He whispered, "*Goddess . . .*"

"*Terryn!*"

There was no light. Yet somehow Terryn's vision clarified.

He whirled where he knelt to face the opening of the tunnel. Someone stood there. Larger than life. His eyes were wild, his hair loose and snarled. His chest was bare and scarred with many open cuts which ran black with shade-blighted blood.

"*Terryn,*" Fendrel said, "*take my hand.*"

CHAPTER 17

A BLAST OF DARKNESS LIKE SPEWING ASH HIT AYLETH and sent her flying backwards. She landed hard on the statue's wrist and skidded over the curve and down toward the drop. Only the frantic impulses of survival instinct made her scrabble wildly with hands and feet, trying to catch hold. The polished stone surface offered almost no grip, but by some wild chance or divine providence, the fingers of her shackled right hand managed to catch in a small fracture.

Her lower body dangled out over the huge drop. The tiered steps of the idol mound spun wildly below her, and the whole of Dulìmurian seemed to gyrate under her dazed vision. Her legs kicked wildly, searching for purchase in the empty air. Her torso screamed with pain from her broken ribs, but she hardly felt that pain through the lightning-like explosions of panic flashing in her brain.

The air around her swirled with *oblivis* and the discordant reverberations of a spell song—the *Cravan Druch* working its dire magic to extend a life that should be ended.

"Ayleth!"

The voice was scarcely discernible through the spell song battering her ears. Ayleth looked up, blinking as motes of *oblivis* flew like sand across her face and stung her eyes. Somehow, impossibly, a face clarified above her.

"Ayleth!" Gerard threw himself onto his stomach across the statue's wrist.

How could he be here? How? It must be some sort of illusion, some sort of nightmare. It couldn't be real. But that was his beautiful face scored by the ugly red wounds of the Warpwitch's curse blast. Those were his golden eyes flashing with terror and courage mingled into one unnamable emotion. No dream could depict him in such perfect detail.

He slid on his stomach, stretching down across the curve of the wrist, reaching for her.

"No." Ayleth gagged on her own voice but forced it out of her fear-clenched throat. "No, don't!" Her fingers strained to hold onto that tiny protrusion in the smooth stone, and her muscles jumped with pain. "You'll fall!"

He didn't listen. He slid further until she thought he would surely lose whatever tentative hold he had and fall headfirst out into empty air. But no matter how far he stretched, he could not reach her. Even if he did, he'd never find leverage enough to pull her up.

"Get back, Gerard!" Ayleth screamed at him. Her ribcage was on fire. She felt her grip giving way. The oblidite she held onto cracked. She had seconds left, if even that. "Get away from here!"

Odile would revive. The *Cravan Druch* would see to that. She would revive, and when she did, she would do to Gerard what she'd done to his father. Ayleth saw again the powerful figure of the king collapsed in that small vaulted crypt with a black hole blasted through his heart. She couldn't bear for that to happen again—not to Gerard. He was the Golden Prince. The betrayal she'd felt before, the disappointment and disgust, all of it vanished from her heart. If she believed nothing else, she *knew* that Gerard was the promise of the Goddess fulfilled. He would, he *must* sit on the throne of Perrinion and guide his people into a new age of peace and harmony. It *must* happen or else . . . or else . . .

Or else her death was for nothing. Her death, the deaths of her brothers and sisters, Terryn's death, and their mutual and inevitable damnation. All that loss, all that pain, all that eternity of torment could only be made right if Gerard lived.

He stared down into her eyes, reading her desperate expression. She watched his features harden, his brow drawing into a stern line. He bit out something she couldn't hear, a curse perhaps, then disappeared from her view, scrambling backwards.

Ayleth choked on a sob, half hope, half despair. Had he understood? Had he realized all that she could not find the words or the breath to say? Was he even now fleeing back across the idol's outstretched arm?

She slipped. The miniscule grip she'd managed to find with her left hand broke free. Only her right hand still held on. In a moment of pure desperation, she cried out in her soul, "*Laranta!*" The shout rippled down the soul tether, down beneath the barriers of iron poison, reaching her shade where she crouched in isolated pain.

Laranta responded at once. She lurched up, flinging herself against the iron suppressions. Ayleth felt the jolt of agony burst through her shade's spirit. But she gave everything she could. She channeled her magic along the soul tether, offering up all the strength remaining to her. It wasn't much. But for now . . .

Setting her jaw, Ayleth pulled her left hand back as far as the chain links would allow, then drove it, fingers first, into the stone with enough force to chip away a small chunk, creating a handhold. This she gripped with all her might. Just in time, for in that very moment, her right hand gave out. The iron links binding her hands together clashed.

Laranta poured more strength into her, fighting for all

she was worth against the suppressions. Ayleth reached down inside her mind, her soul, trying to take hold of that power, shuddering as Laranta's agonized howl echoed in her head. *"Come, Laranta!"* she begged. *"Just a little more!"*

She lifted her right hand up to the farthest extent the chains would allow and, once again, drove her fingers into the stone. It wasn't much of a grip, but it was something.

Using her stomach muscles, she tried to pull her feet up. But though she could get her toes to scrape the underside of the wrist, she couldn't find any footing and couldn't get them up far enough to make a difference.

Laranta's howl faltered. The soul tether shivered with her pain. The iron was driving her back again.

"Laranta! Laranta, please!"

Mistress, the voice reached her senses, a fading whisper. *Mistress . . .*

"Ayleth!"

She looked up. Gerard was above her again, his face ghostly in the *oblivis*-thickened air. "Grab hold!" he shouted, and she saw that he was extending something toward her hands. It took her a few blinks to realize what it was: the hilt of a sword. His hands, wrapped in rags cut from his own shirt, gripped the blade with fierce determination.

She stared up at his face. Blood dripped down his beautiful features, running from the unhealed wounds. His eyes flashed, and his jaw strained as he clenched his bared teeth. There was no way he could hold onto that blade. There was no way he could pull her up. And yet . . . and yet . . .

Ayleth lunged up to catch the hilt, beyond heeding the agony in her ribcage. She expected Gerard to lose his grip, to let her fall. His face twisted, but his hold did not falter. She gripped tight and, using the last of Laranta's strength, managed to haul herself farther up the curve of the wrist, finding other small handholds, and soon footholds as well. Then Gerard reached out and grabbed the back of her shirt, heaving her up beside him. She collapsed flat on her face, breathing hard.

Before her brain had a chance to come to grips with the reality of her own survival, Gerard grabbed her shoulder. His hands, rag-wrapped and bleeding, yanked her roughly upright, turning her to face him. "Kill her, Ayleth," he breathed. His voice wasn't even audible over the clamor of the *Cravan Druch* ringing through the air. But she didn't need to hear him to understand. She could read the urgency in his eyes. "Kill her now."

He pushed the sword into her hands. Its blade and hilt were black and polished to a brilliant shine. Oblidite, she realized. But there was no time to wonder how Gerard had come by such a weapon. She staggered to her feet, turned, and drew a quick breath.

Then she ran up the slope of the massive hand. Carrying the sword was awkward with her hands shackled, but she managed it, adjusting her grip as she gained the top of the curve and looked down into the cupped palm.

Odile's body lay in a pool of black, flowing blood. But the blood flowed in the wrong direction, streaming over the stone into the gory wound of the neck. Threads of *oblivis* stretched out from the shoulders, gripping the severed head, pulling it back. The long, blood-matted hair trailed on the stone behind it.

Ayleth stared at that face twisted in a horrified mask of pain. For an instant she froze in place, transfixed by that sight. The mouth hung wide, the tongue protruding, bloated and purple. The eyes were rolled back so that only the whites showed. The *Cravan Druch* thundered around them, sustaining life that should not live.

The eyelids blinked. The eyes focused, moved. Fixed on Ayleth. Full of awareness.

A bolt of pure terror shot through Ayleth's soul. Galvanized into action, she slid down the sloping heel of the hand, lifting the sword high as she went. She gripped it by the hilt, blade pointed down, and aimed a blow that should skewer the headless woman's heart. A wild roar burst from her lips as she brought the blade down.

But as the point plunged for its mark, the oblidite melted away. A cloud of whirling black motes flew up into Ayleth's eyes, and her shackled hands were left gripping empty air. Odile, still bleeding at the neck, her throat a mass of black spell threads, blinked up at Ayleth. Her mouth twisted, her tongue writhing wildly between her lips.

Ayleth, weaponless, attacked her with fingers curled, ready to grab and break and tear. But before she could take hold, Odile's hand came up, and a blast of *oblivis* burst in Ayleth's face. It was not as great a blast as the last one—there was an uncertain, unfocused quality to the magic. But it was strong enough to send Ayleth flying back into one of the upraised finger pillars.

She struck hard and fell to the ground, for the moment too stunned to move, to even lift her head.

Odile rose to her feet. *Oblivis* surrounded her in a dense, churning cloud. She staggered, nearly fell, and caught her balance. Her head lolled weirdly as the *Cravan Druch* spell threads strengthened. Her eyes rolled, fixing her gaze at last on Ayleth with an intensity hot enough to kill. Hatred raged in that gaze, mingled with horror. And longing. And love.

Odile raised both hands. Her eyes swirled with the blackness of her spirit, with the warring of the terrible emotions festering in her core. "I'm sorry, Olena," she said.

Oblivis burst from her hands in two jagged lances. But they both went wide, one striking the ground just to Ayleth's right, the other flashing over her shoulder and hitting the finger pillar behind her. The pillar cracked, crumbled, and fell under that blow. Ayleth ducked, covering her head, but looked up again almost at once, peering through the swirling motes and haze of magic, desperate to see what could have thrown off Odile's aim, already suspecting what she would find.

Gerard. He had no weapon, so he'd thrown himself bodily into Odile, wrapping his arms around her, pinning her arms to her sides. He had no magic, no shade, barely any mortal strength left to him after having breathed in so much *oblivis*. He had nothing but the strength of his own mortal body, yet he wrenched, pulled, dragged Odile toward the edge of the hand.

What was he doing? Was he trying to wrestle her out into the empty air, trying to drag her with him over the side? He knew that even a fall like that couldn't kill her. But it might be enough to spare Ayleth, enough to give Ayleth a chance to kill her later.

"Gerard, no!" Ayleth screamed.

Odile snarled out a curse. Then she opened her mouth wide, unnaturally wide, and *oblivis* streamed from her throat in a sinuous coil, looped behind her head, and wrapped around Gerard's throat. Another command, and it hardened and yanked Gerard away from Odile. He tried to maintain his hold but couldn't, caught as he was in that snake-like grasp of darkness.

Odile stumbled two steps forward, then twisted to face her attacker. She drew herself up tall like the queen she was, and her hair streamed black behind her, caught in the storm of *oblivis*. "I know your face," she said, her voice velvet smooth and full of poison. "You can only be your father's son. So! The Chosen King finds ways to persecute me even from beyond the crypt."

She stepped forward, her footfalls tentative, her head still loose on her mended neck. Stretching out one hand, she touched Gerard's flinching face, caressed his cheekbone. Her hard nail drew a fresh line of blood to go with the other marks. "Tell me, little princeling, what have you done to my lieutenant? What have you done to my sweet Inren? Did you slaughter her even as your father slaughtered so many of my faithful servants?"

Gerard couldn't answer. His mouth opened, but only in a desperate gasp for air. The *oblivis* lifted him off his feet. He was helpless in its grip. Odile moved her arm in a sharp, flinging gesture, and the *oblivis* swung him out between the index finger and thumb pillars, suspending him over the city far below.

"The prophesied gift of the Goddess, come to the mortal world," Odile mused, watching Gerard kick like a condemned man dancing in a hangman's noose. Her smile flashed. When she spoke again, blood and spittle flew through her teeth. "Your Goddess's gifts are not worth having."

Ayleth watched, her spirit frozen, her body petrified like the *oblivis*-blasted fringe forest. Time slowed to a measure of heartbeats, each a sharp stab in her breast.

One beat, and she saw Gerard's eyes widen, saw him realize the certainty of his doom.

A second beat . . . and she felt something pull at her awareness. A throb of magic, of power.

On the third beat, she turned and gazed, not with her mortal eyes but with her spirit, into the utter darkness of the Presence rising to hover within the center of the *eitr* crown. She saw there the terrible potency anchored to the world of matter via that living metal it possessed.

It looked at her. It beckoned.

Oromor whispered in her ear: ***Now, now, now.***

Her heart pounded a fourth beat.

Odile flicked her hand. The coil around Gerard's

throat disintegrated to nothing. Ayleth dived forward, propelling herself with her legs, sliding on her stomach across the smooth contours of the palm. Gerard's scream tore through her ears and faded into distance.

She caught the crown in both hands. She did not notice how it burned her skin. She did not notice the shock of pain shooting through her bones, shooting through her senses, bursting in her brain. She noticed only how easy it was to lift that massive circlet of living metal and bring it down onto her head.

CHAPTER 18

IT MUST BE AN ILLUSION. A DESPERATE ILLUSION invented by a mind lost to insanity as it strove against the final death throes overcoming its physical body. But it was the only visible thing in this dark, scorching world. So, though he wanted to look away, Terryn could do nothing but stare.

Fendrel took a step closer. That single action was enough to jolt Terryn into reality. Fendrel was his enemy. He stood up and backed away.

"*Stop!*" Fendrel barked.

Terryn felt the edge of the pit under his heel. One more step and he would fall, joining Nisirdi in that boiling blackness. The tar was rising anyway and gathering in thicker strands to fall streaming from the ceiling above. Soon it would make no difference whether he stood his ground or fell.

But Fendrel's eyes pleaded silently. He stretched out one trembling hand, which ran with blackened blood. More blood poured from the cuts across his torso—cuts Terryn recognized from when Fendrel performed the purging spell on Ayleth.

"*What . . . what are you doing?*" Terryn demanded.

"*What does it look like I'm doing?*" Fendrel snarled. "*I'm saving your ungrateful hide.*" He took another step, this one more cautious than the last. His face was pale with loss of blood, his bare skin white where it showed through the streaming stains of blackened blood. "*Come to me, boy. Take my hand. I can get you out of here.*"

Terryn shook his head. "*You want me dead. Dead and damned. I know you too well, Fendrel. I won't fall for your tricks.*"

Fendrel swallowed hard. He didn't speak, but neither

did his outstretched hand waver.

"*You ordered my death,*" Terryn said. "*You looked me in the eye and declared me worthless. Worthless to the Order. Worthless to the Goddess.*" He ground his teeth. "*Worthless to you.*" The air was so hot that his skin began to blister, to sear like meat over a fire pit. He shuddered, gasped. Tears streamed down his cheeks, burning as they went.

And yet he could not make himself look away from that hard, unreadable face. That face he had trusted above all others. His master who had trained him in the secret ways of the Order. His savior who had pulled him from the rubble of Cró Ular. The man who had taken him under his wing, given him shelter, given him purpose, given him everything that he was.

His killer.

"*I have seen through your lies—all of them,*" Terryn spat. A stream of burning tar fell in a curtain between them, but Fendrel passed through it as though it wasn't there, closing the distance between them. Terryn drew back a fraction more. His lips pulled back in a twisted grimace of pain. "*We are not the servants of the Goddess. We chase down and slaughter Her creation. We don't act in holiness, only fear.*

Evander's fear. The fear that drives all humanity to subdue and oppress rather than to nurture and liberate. It is fear, not faith, which has shaped us, twisted us, transformed us into monsters far worse than those we hunted."

Was that a flicker of emotion in those iron-hard eyes? A tremor running through that extended hand and arm?

The darkness closed in, and the heat drew a moan of pain from Terryn's throat. But the pressure of final words rose straight from his gut, heaving like sickness across his tongue. *"I will never be your heir, Fendrel,"* he said. *"I will never be what you want."*

For a moment, silence burned between them, filled with the hazy ripple of boiling air. Terryn's vision swam, darkened. He sank to his knees. But he would not let his gaze break from Fendrel's. Not now, not at the very end.

Fendrel's face jolted suddenly, his head twisting sharply to one side. The blood streaming from his torso seemed to increase, running as swiftly as the tar flowing down the walls. He pulled his head up, his eyes flashing. *"That's where you're wrong,"* he said.

Terryn wasn't fast enough. Though he tried to turn, to fling himself into the pit, his limbs refused to obey him.

Perhaps his own despair slowed his reflexes. Perhaps the loss of Nisirdi had weakened him too much. Perhaps he simply never was as quick or as strong as his master.

Just as tar fell from the ceiling above in a deluge of burning blackness, Fendrel wrapped his arms around Terryn, shielding him with his bleeding body. Heat, pure heat, overwhelmed all senses except the stench of burning flesh. And then a voice spoke in Terryn's ear:

"Whatever you do . . . wherever you go . . . you will always be my son."

Then Fendrel's scream exploded in Terryn's head.

The Anathema threads burst in an explosion of magic, knocking Hollis flat on her back. For a moment, she stared up at the dizzyingly distant sky. Actual sky, she realized. A break in the *oblivis* atmosphere. And beyond it glimmered tiny pinpoints of light. For a moment, she couldn't remember what they were called. Then dully, distantly, she thought, *Oh, yes. Stars . . .*

But there was no time to dwell on far-off beauty. She rolled over and pushed up on her elbows. "Fendrel?" Her heart thudded wildly in her throat. Her shade had retreated, frightened by the explosion of magic, limiting Hollis to her mortal vision. The world was dark, and she struggled to discern anything. But her eyes slowly adjusted.

"Fendrel!" She scrambled up onto her hands and knees and crawled over Terryn's prone body to reach the figure fallen beside him. She pressed her hand against Fendrel's breast, and his blighted blood burned under her palm. "No, no, no," she whimpered, pulling his head into her lap. Was he dead already? Was his spirit torn free and damned?

"Come to me! Come to me!" she screamed to her shade deep down in her soul. But it did not answer.

She gazed down into that face, that face she knew even better than her own though she'd scarcely glimpsed it in twenty years. He was almost unrecognizable now. Blackened veins bulged through his skin, and his open eyes, staring vacantly up at the sky, were black orbs without even a gleam of white remaining. No trace of the stormy gray eyes that had once so captivated her heart.

Hollis's arms shuddered so violently that she could

hardly hold onto him. But hold him she did, pressing his head to her breast and rocking slowly back and forth. In that moment, he wasn't the man she now knew him to be. He wasn't the Venator Dominus, the Legend of the Witch Wars. The liar. In that moment, that final moment, he was only Fendrel. The boy she'd loved. The boy she'd lost, not to any monster but to himself. The boy who had wholeheartedly chased down his own damnation.

Hollis gritted her teeth as she wiped strands of sweaty hair back from his forehead. Then she closed her eyes and leaned down, pressing a kiss to those swollen black lips. She tasted *oblivis*. And death.

An explosion of light and sound burst suddenly in the darkness behind her eyelids. She opened her eyes but saw only the brilliance of light and, through that light, the pounding force of magnificent wings. Not the multitude of wings that was her own shade. No . . . these wings were much greater, and when they moved, they shed spears of light in bursts of color that dazzled the spirit. And with every burst, another note of wild, indescribable song rang in her ears. Hollis tried to shut her eyes, but she couldn't. Her mortal eyes were already shut, and her spirit couldn't help seeing this power manifest before her. She stared in open-mouthed wonder as those wings rose into the air, carrying a sinuous body swiftly toward a red, leering slash in reality.

The Haunts were opening.

The chaotic silence of that realm clashed against the brilliant light-song, nearly overwhelming Hollis's senses. She clung harder to Fendrel's empty host body, knowing there was nothing she could do to save him now. Spirits appeared above her, trailing broken tethers. She knew them at once—the many-limbed and hideous Anathema that had been Fendrel's companion for many years, and that glow, that golden soul-orb it clutched in its claws . . . was Fendrel himself. She would know him anywhere.

"Please," she whispered. "Please, Goddess . . ."

The winged being, the creature of light, flashed straight for the hellish gate, straight for those souls as they were sucked through. The Haunts began to shut, like a mouth closing in a hard, toothy grin of satisfaction. The being's wings pulsed one last time, and a flash of blinding brilliance made Hollis scream and duck her head, pressing her face against Fendrel's lifeless cheek. The cacophony of music and dreadful silence resounded in her head, deafening her spirit.

Then all was still.

Hollis opened her eyes, her mortal eyes. Dark specks and bright dots danced along the edges of her vision but could not veil the sight of Fendrel's dead face in her lap. She drew a shuddering breath, and three tears fell from her cheeks, landed on his face, and trailed down into his beard. Another breath, and she lifted her head.

Terryn met her gaze.

He knelt before her, holding Fendrel's hand, tears tracking down his cheeks. His torso was bloody with the long, shallow cuts of Fendrel's cleansing magic. But the blood flowing down his chest and stomach was red, clean. In his eyes she saw light shining—the same light she had seen in the sky above, flashing up to the open Haunts. The same song, shimmering with magic. That light and song was his shade—his ascendant, unfettered shade. And he had used it, used that incredible power in a last attempt to reach and rescue Fendrel's soul from the Haunts.

Hollis wanted to speak, but she could find no words.

She couldn't ask the question she longed to ask. *Did your shade succeed? Did you get him? Did you save him?*

Terryn looked her in the eye, but she couldn't read his expression.

"Terryn! Are you all right?" Venator Kephan approached, offering a hand. Terryn accepted it, allowing the venator to pull him to his feet. He swayed and looked as though he might topple but managed to right himself. The other Evanderians drew near, looking uneasy. Fendrel had given orders that Terryn be killed only the night before. Now here he stood above the dead body of their Dominus, and they didn't know what to think.

But Kephan stood close to Terryn's side, his stance slightly protective. "I thought you were done for," he said, looking from Terryn's bleeding chest down to Fendrel on the ground. "He . . . I guess in the end he—"

Before Kephan could finish whatever he was about to say, a blast of power rippled across the land. A wave of magic so profound, even mortal eyes could see it with no need for shadow vision. It toppled Terryn and the Evanderians from their feet, knocked Hollis flat on the ground, dragged Fendrel out of her arms, and sent his body rolling several yards away.

The shade-taken horde of Odile began to scream. Picking themselves up from wherever the blast had flung them, they scattered into the dark shadows of the Witchwood and away. Hollis pulled back upright and stared in the direction the blast had come from. "Haunts damn!" she breathed.

The wall of vines was gone. Simply gone.

Nothing stood in her way, nothing blocked her view of the ruinous city. Nothing impeded her gaze as she looked down the long, broken street to the city's center, where the broken idol knelt on its monolith, the hand raised high and blazing with red light, as though it had just caught a dying sun as it fell to the earth.

"Ayleth." Hollis leaped to her feet. "Ayleth!"

A flash of movement, a flicker of glowing wings. Hollis turned and saw Terryn break into a run, heading straight for the idol. She could almost see the white, shining dragon following in the air behind him.

CHAPTER 19

TIME CEASED. OR SIMPLY NEVER WAS.

Ayleth stood in a place of perfect stillness. Not darkness, for darkness required an absence of light, and there was no such thing as light. Somewhere far away, something burned. Her head. Her skin, her hair. Unyielding metal clamped down around her skull, and power scorched through it, lightning branches of magic. She felt it, felt her mouth opening, her throat constricting, her lungs heaving as she screamed with pain.

But none of that mattered. Not here.

Here was simply silence. Void without distance. Without form save for her own individual personhood trapped in the center of nothing. She was the entirety of everything that existed, a lonely, solitary universe.

But then . . . a feeling. Not her own.

A Presence.

Delight.

A blaze of sudden life and brilliance and sound exploded through her senses. Ayleth tried to put up her hands, to shut her eyes, to block it out. But she possessed neither hands nor eyes here, nothing with which to stop the onslaught. Delight coursed through her, coiled around her soul. She felt dark tendrils grasping hold of her vision, opening it wider, sending her gaze deeper. Down into a darkness of spirit and existence utterly foreign to her. Memories . . .

She saw the world alive beneath a new white sun, a world that shimmered and glowed, its rivers running with *eitr*, its mountains tall and blue and alive. She saw great cities grow, rising from the ground like projections of crystal and ice. They reverberated with music, with spell songs more complex and varied and beautiful and dreadful than any of the paltry melodies she'd ever picked out on her bone pipes.

Ages passed. The cities rose into the air, moving across the surface of the world like stars tracing their paths in the heavens above, rising through the atmosphere, floating free into the deep darkness of the night. Beings soared between them, beings formed of matter, shimmering souls only just contained within those cage-like host bodies. They traveled through air and space in carriages Ayleth could not describe, machines formed of fire and magic and living *eitr*. The beings that rode them, that controlled them, were glorious beyond imagination.

She tried to speak. She had no mouth, but she tried to form the word, a word her mortal language could scarcely contain: *Ildrir*.

She blinked . . .

. . . and more ages were come and gone. She saw the cities fall, the shining towers collapsing in balls of fire from the sky, striking the earth, and sending shockwaves of destruction. The *eitr* rivers poured down through crevices, sinking to the depths of the world, swallowed up by the furnace at its core. Spirits coursed through the air, screaming their spell songs, all the various colors of the shade spectrum flashing in the darkness.

Ayleth felt sorrow. She felt rage. Despair. None of it her own, yet it flowed through her, as real as the blood in her veins. The Haunts opened wide. Not the small cracks in reality she had witnessed numerous times. No. Amid the chaos, that yawning mouth opened as though to devour the whole of the world. Ayleth felt herself being drawn, dragged. She screamed and thrashed, but this was not her memory, so she could not fight it. Inexorably, the dark soul surrounding her pulled her with it into an eternity of torment.

Here, there was no self. Only crushing. Only horror upon horror without time or hope of ending. *Oblivis* surrounded her, but she could not control it, could not manipulate it to her desired purpose, for she had neither desires nor purpose. She was cut off. Cut off from the very Song of Life that had chorused in her spirit from the moment her existence began—although she had never realized it, never acknowledged it.

Here, there was no great and abiding Song.

What was that?

Something became real, became visible. A crack in eternity, a mere sliver of light. But her being, her sense of self, suddenly coalesced in a jolt of desperate need. She lunged toward that opening and fell through, back into an existence of time in which nothing was unending, neither love nor loss, neither horror nor hope. A world of constant change.

But this wasn't the world she had left behind when the Haunts claimed her soul. This was a small, confined world. A world of *eitr*, living but limited. The mind here was too different from her own, the memories too strange. An inanimate host body in which a soul could anchor but never truly live.

She flung herself at the boundaries of this host, seeking to tear her way free. The relief of escaping the Haunts faded in the light of this new imprisonment. Someone had drawn her here and trapped her. And for what purpose?

There was a pulse of red through the *eitr*. Something mortal amid the immortal blue glow. A mind appeared as though from nowhere. A mortal mind with a pattern of thoughts and memories and desires and fears and lusts and longings. It was still a limited mind, but it was at least *more* akin to that which she had known in those ages long ago. She poured herself into that mind, relieved to find something over which she might assume control. She peered through mortal eyes into a world of matter, nowhere near as glorious as the *eitr*-rich world she had known of old, but exciting in its possibilities. A world ripe for conquest.

Then, just as she began to extend her power from within the confines of the crown, to take control of this mortal mind, bindings clamped down. Another spirit rose to meet her.

Oromor, spoke a voice which she knew.

Irimir, she answered. But it wasn't her voice which spoke. It was the Dark One possessing her.

With no other word spoken between them, the spirits threw themselves at one another in a clash of wills and power and magic and song. A terrible battle which lasted both a hundred years and a single instant. But at its end, she—Oromor—fell beneath the strength of her sister. She became subservient.

More sights played out before her vision, faster and faster, too swift to fathom. Ayleth watched the rise and fall of empires—mortal empires this time, mortal cities from legend and history. Some of them she recognized from things she'd been taught as a child. Most she did not. It didn't matter. She wasn't Ayleth now. She was Oromor. She lived and pulsed Oromor.

At last Irimir's presence withdrew, leaving behind emptiness, loneliness that was a welcome relief. She felt the *eitr* crown pass from head to head. Some of the minds she was able to overtake, but most died in the overtaking, destroyed too quickly to be of any lasting use. Without the right blood, they snuffed out like candles, sometimes within days, sometimes within moments.

Ayleth lived Oromor's frustration as it sought to work beyond the restrictions of its *eitr* prison. She felt its power so ancient, its sentience so foreign and profound. She spun through centuries of darkness punctuated by bursts of power followed by more darkness.

And she felt the moment when Odile took the crown. Oromor's ecstasy and agony were her own as it recognized the blood that would allow this mortal host to survive, but also the contrasting and enslaving might of Irimir. And so, the centuries of servitude began again.

When the *atacara* struck, it was like a gift of lightning. Ayleth lived that moment, and her soul exalted in the power flowing through her—power enough to overcome her enslavers, power enough to take ascendancy and control. But just at the last, just when everything she longed for—everything Oromor longed for—was within her grasp—

Odile cast the crown from her head.

Still, the potency of the *atacara* rushed through her being. She must channel it, use it, find a way to make it serve her purpose. First, she strained at the confines of her *eitr* prison—but that was no use. If she escaped this host, she had only the Haunts waiting to claim her. No, she must somehow work to influence the world through the host she had.

She reached into the Haunts themselves and pulled *oblivis* into the mortal world. Massive tides of darkness ran between realities, and the Witchwood grew up, covering the landscape. Ayleth-as-Oromor extended herself out through a winding network of parasitic vines, shooting through the tortured trees, racing to swallow up all this world.

But always, always, her will was thwarted. Rivers of holy water touched by a source of light beyond her influence hemmed her in on all sides save one. And that one side, where she ought to have been able to pour forth in all her rage and might, held a barrier—a spell too powerful even for the last echoes of the *atacara* reverberating in her soul to overcome.

Desperation. Limitation. Frustration and wrath. Mere mortal words failed to describe the tumult of feeling that tore through her, ready to shred her awareness. Mortal words could only describe mortal emotions. Here, they were without context. Her mind bent and threatened to break.

Ayleth screamed.

With that scream, the spirit inside her retracted somewhat, and Ayleth found room for her mind to exist. Pulling herself forward into awareness of time, awareness of the present, she realized that everything she just experienced had taken place inside her head in less than the space of a single breath. She tried to look at Oromor, at the huge Presence in her head, but it was too great, too powerful for her mind to give a projected form. It simply would not be contained. But she felt the awful *personality* of it.

It seemed to smile.

Ayleth felt her mortal body, still crouched on that platform hand of oblidite. Her shackled hands were still on the crown, still holding it as she placed it on her head. She needed to throw it off. Now. While she still had some control of her own will.

Stretch out your hand.

There was meaning in her head without words. Her mind shuddered with the effort to understand.

Stretch out your hand, mortal. See what I can give to you.

Another instant. Enough time for Ayleth to blink.

She was back in the present, kneeling on oblidite, staring across the palm to where Odile was still turning to look back at her, her mouth still shaping into a scream of "*No!*" Her hand rising, power mounting for an attack.

Ayleth saw the empty space behind Odile where Gerard had been suspended only a moment before.

She threw out her right hand, hardly aware of any conscious choice on her part. She scarcely noticed when the action broke the iron chains that had bound her all this time and they fell clattering to the ground, freeing her from the iron influence. She scarcely noticed when Laranta reacted deep inside her, surging in an upswelling of Feral magic.

Darkness streamed out from her fingertips—*oblivis* gathered into a long, concentrated coil. She felt its attraction to her will, felt it swarm to her and then burst out from her hand, streaking past Odile. It was like her own arm, like an extension of herself reaching, stretching. She sensed the rush of wind as the *oblivis* raced against time, raced against gravity itself.

She could not see him, but she *felt* Gerard below her, twisting and turning as he plummeted toward the city far below.

She could not see, but she *felt* when she caught him in a twist of *oblivis*.

The breath was knocked from his lungs, but she was gentle. She was in control—more control than she ought to possess, a distant part of her mind protested. She pulled him up through the empty air, back up to the idol's palm, between the finger and thumb.

Ayleth blinked her awareness back inside her own head. Her skin burned, and she felt the pain, but it simply didn't matter. She stared at Odile, who stood across from her, a storm of *oblivis* gripped in a whorl around her fist. Odile made no move as Ayleth dropped Gerard onto the platform behind her, then placed herself between him and the Witch Queen like a mother bear standing guard over her cub.

Odile still made no move. Her face pale with dread, she stared at Ayleth, at the crown on her head. "Olena," she said. "Olena, I have to believe you're still in there. I have to believe you can hear me."

Ayleth braced herself, raising both hands. *Oblivis* gathered at her command. It was so easy. So natural, as if she'd been born with this power. It was her di Mauvalis blood, her birthright.

"Olena!" Odile's face twisted with entreaty. "Take off the crown. Now. While you still can."

"Why would I do that, Grandmother? So you can blast me to oblivion?"

"Better to die than to lose your soul to that fiend." Odile took a step, her hands still up, the churning *oblivis* around her building in power, ready to explode. But she restrained it for the moment. "Oromor will consume you. You will lose everything to its will."

"Everything?" Ayleth laughed, a hollow sound that echoed in her chest where her heart ought to beat. "I have lost everything already."

She saw Terryn's face as the death blow struck. She saw Hollis's face as she revealed her many lies. She saw Fendrel's face as he bound her in iron mitts. As the Red Hoods gathered around her, as they declared her sentence of death and cast her from their Order.

Deep, deep down inside her, behind Oromor's tumultuous power, she thought she heard a voice cry out, *Mistress! Mistress, wait!*

But she shook her head and focused her gaze on Odile, her brows drawn tight under the burning band of the crown. "But I can make certain that you lose with me," she said.

They struck at the same moment.

Oblivis blasts collided in a terrible clash that should

have sent Ayleth careening backwards. But she braced herself and stood strong. She felt Oromor's power coursing through her physical body, beyond anything she'd ever before experienced. The Feral magic she'd known all her life was as nothing compared to this. But Odile was a match for her. More than a match—Ayleth felt it at once. The shade Odile carried was the greater of the two, if not by much. And there was no *atacara* song spell to augment Oromor's might.

But Odile's body was weakened, held together only by the *Cravan Druch*, while Ayleth's body was young and strong.

The idol's hand shook under the force of the crashing element. Its remaining fingers swayed, and the whole arm threatened to come toppling down. Both Odile and Ayleth backed up, retracting their powers. Odile looked nervous, Ayleth noted. She must be afraid to die in a fall, for if Ayleth caused the fall, such a death should be sufficient to break the *Cravan Druch*.

"You're afraid, Grandmother," she said. She believed it was her own voice speaking, but she wasn't sure. "How long has it been since you felt real fear? Since the Chosen

King marched on Dulìmurian? No . . . no, I don't believe you were afraid, not even then. You always had a plan, always had a maneuver to protect yourself against your enemy. You always had an excuse for your own self-preservation. So why would you fear?"

Odile took a careful step to her left, her eyes fixed intently on Ayleth. Ayleth moved in perfect synchronization with her. They circled each other around the center of the palm. *Oblivis* followed them both in a maelstrom of glittering darkness.

"Olena," Odile said, "this is not you speaking. You think it is, but you are wrong. It is already inside your head. It is already taking you over. If you fight, if you try . . . you might still save yourself. There's something of you present still. I can see you in your eyes."

Ayleth subtly put out a finger of power, reaching, stretching, searching for something in the dark. She took a slice of *oblivis* and hardened it into stone. "I don't think you've known true fear in many years," she said, her voice pure venom. "Not since before you took this crown for yourself. Not since before you became the New Goddess, the Poison. Not since . . ."

She paused. Part of her didn't want to go on, didn't want to speak the malicious words forming on her tongue. But another part of her, a much greater part, urged her on. Her mouth moved and words poured out against her will. "You've not felt fear since they took your daughter. Since they bound her to a stake. Since they struck the flint, and the fire took hold, and she screamed for you to come—"

Odile roared. Another horrible burst of power flew at Ayleth, a storm of wrath and magic. She was only just fast enough to put up her hand, only just fast enough to shield herself from a blow that surely would have torn her mortal body into a million pieces. The blow shattered against a shield of oblidite instead, unable to penetrate. But it kept coming, coming, coming.

Ayleth's feet skidded on the surface of the palm. Inch by inch she moved toward the edge and the fatal drop awaiting. She stared through the storm. Her mortal eyes could see nothing but churning, blinding clouds of *oblivis*. But her shadow sight pierced through all and met Odile's gaze.

She saw fear.

She saw sorrow.

She saw rage.

She saw herself. Her own mirror image. The monster. The woman. The murderer.

The Venatrix.

A surge of hatred burst through her soul. But beneath the hate—which she distantly realized might not be entirely hers—was another feeling. An agony she hardly dared acknowledge. She turned away from that feeling and focused all the hatred in her soul into Odile's eyes. Odile stared back, more than Ayleth's equal.

Then her eyes widened.

A figure moved through the *oblivis,* coming suddenly at Odile from behind her right shoulder. His limbs were wrapped in darkness, and in his hands he gripped an oblidite sword. He moved beyond his own control, completely at the mercy of the *oblivis* holding him in its grip.

The *oblivis* Ayleth controlled.

It was Ayleth who raised his right arm, lifting the sword high.

Ayleth smiled.

"*But I will send a champion,*" she murmured. "*I will send the man whom I have chosen to cut off the Poison's head.*"

Realization flooded Odile's face. Just at the last instant, she turned.

The blade swung, connecting with a thick thud.

Bone snapped. Muscles tore. Blood flowed in a shade-blighted fountain.

Odile's head fell and rolled.

A burst of violently liberated magic exploded out from her ruined body. The mortal spirit, bound fast by witchcraft to that of her shade, spun wildly free, sending flashes of light and darkness rippling through the ether. The body teetered and collapsed. The spirits roared through the churning *oblivis* storm, leaving a trail of soul fire in their wake, too swift even for the Haunts to catch.

And the *Cravan Druch* strained and broke in a torrent of shattering spell song.

CHAPTER 20

THE GRIP OF OBLIVIS ABRUPTLY RELAXED, AND GERARD dropped hard onto the oblidite. He covered his head with his hands and curled up into a ball as wave upon wave of darkness rolled out from the headless body standing right beside him. The oblidite beneath him shivered with inner tremors, and the hand itself swayed dangerously in the air. At any moment it would crack, and he would once more face that terrible plunge from which he'd only just been saved.

This time, there would be no miraculous rescue.

His arms ached, their bones reverberating from the force of the blow he'd delivered. He realized that his hands still gripped the hilt of the sword. His ears rang with an ongoing pounding pulse unlike anything he'd ever before heard, and the air seemed heavy as it struck him blow after blow. But the force of those blows, though enough to make him wince and cry out, lessened with each wave, and at last he managed to open his eyes.

He found himself facing Odile. Her head lay before him, mouth open, eyes gaping. This time, no spirit looked out from those dead black disks.

Gerard's hand tightened around the sword hilt. Only then did he realize that the vibrations in his arms originated from it. It still reverberated from the blow he'd struck. When he tried to let go, his fingers wouldn't obey.

This was it. This was the moment.

The moment that he'd seen.

He pushed his torso up, twisting to look back over his shoulder, knowing exactly what sight awaited him.

Ayleth stood in the center of a ball of red light. Her hair was aglow, each strand standing out stark like a heated wire, burning, coiling away to ash, and flying off into the sky in a swirling storm. Her skin glowed from the inside, only it wasn't the glow of heat or flame. It was *oblivis*, energized *oblivis*, on the verge of complete combustion. Not black, but red. It should tear her apart. But it didn't. The magic mingled with the blood in her veins, holding her mortal frame together. But it could not protect her mortal soul.

Gerard adjusted his grip on the oblidite sword. Ayleth's attention—rather, the attention of that which gazed out through Ayleth's eyes—was fixed upon the headless body of Odile, glorying in the work she had just accomplished. She did not seem to see Gerard as he got to his feet, as he hauled the sword up once more. As he took the first two steps toward her.

He'd seen every moment of these next few steps in Nilly's vision. Ayleth, lost to the darkness, overcome by the spirit of the crown. He'd seen what she would become—the next Poison. A greater Poison than her grandmother. For there would be no human soul to moderate the ravages of the shade power coursing through her. Ayleth herself, if she was still in there . . .

there was only one thing he could do to save her.

He took a third step.

She turned. She looked at him.

"I'm so sorry," he said, his voice small and thin amid that storm of power.

Her eyelids lowered over her burning red eyes. And when they lifted again an instant later, Gerard thought he saw Ayleth herself looking out at him. Her black eyes, not ringed in pulsing magic but full of humanity and fear and pain. She opened her mouth as though to speak.

Nothing emerged but a scream.

"I'm so sorry, Ayleth!" Gerard gasped. He lifted the sword, and distant starlight glinted off its edge as he swung it for her neck. The blade connected.

But not with its intended target. Instead, it struck Ayleth's upraised hand, hitting hard, yet unable to draw blood. Rather than slicing through flesh and bone, it simply melted away into a spiraling cloud of *oblivis,* which started out black but quickly intensified to raw, raging red.

Ayleth blinked again. Her mouth hung open, still screaming, and dark magic billowed out from her throat. She twisted her hand, and the *oblivis* in the air whorled and caught Gerard by the neck, lifting him into the air so that he kicked and twisted helplessly. He gagged, his hands clawing at his neck, trying to loosen that stranglehold. As he gazed down into Ayleth's face twisted with such pain and such fury, it seemed as though Odile looked back at him.

A voice spoke through her mouth—speaking not in language, but in a harsh sound, like music without the harmony or loveliness of music. It blasted Gerard's senses, plunged into his mind, and he understood it.

You are nothing.

You are nothing.

You are mortal, and you are nothing.

Ayleth slowly closed her hand, curling it tight and squeezing until her knuckles stood out white—until red, energized *oblivis* oozed out between her fingers. The noose around Gerard's neck constricted. He was losing air, but he knew he wouldn't die of strangulation. The *oblivis* would cut right through, severing his head from his body. His eyes bulged. His body convulsed with terror and pain.

Cerine, he thought. He attempted to focus on that

name, strove to pull away from this moment of horror, to see her face in his mind. Her gentle face behind a soft white bridal veil, her eyes so full of wisdom and understanding. And love.

Cerine . . . Cerine . . . .

"Gerard!"

The sound of his name shot through him like a bolt from a crossbow. Gerard swiveled his eyes as far as they would go in their sockets, convinced his ears deceived him. Terryn could not be standing at the crest of the wrist, looking down into the palm of the idol's hand. The red light surrounding Ayleth could not be nearly quenched by the brighter, whiter glow shining in Terryn's eyes.

Ayleth turned, still screaming, still burning. She raised one hand, gathering *oblivis* at her command. But before she could act, Terryn released the magic he held. A beam of light blasted through the *oblivis* cloud, struck Ayleth in the shoulder, and knocked her back against one of the upraised pillar fingers. She fell hard, her body smoking.

The noose of *oblivis* disintegrated. Gerard collapsed, choking and gagging. His vision went black, returned, and went black again. He shook his head, peering across the width of the palm to where Ayleth lay. He expected her to rise, expected her to draw on the power of the shade possessing her. He expected her to slaughter them both in the blink of an eye.

But she didn't rise. She lay flat on her face, her arms outstretched. Her fingers flexed, curled, flexed again, the only sign of life, and the Crown clung to her head, burning her bare scalp.

Terryn slid down the slope of the wrist into the palm. He looked like a nightmare, bloodied and bare-chested, white light glowing in his hands and his chest and his cheeks. He leaped across to Ayleth and without hesitation grabbed her shoulders and pulled her into his arms, rolling her over to look into her face. He reached for the Crown but couldn't touch it, not even with his glowing hands.

Ayleth peered up at him, her eyes burning with fiery *oblivis*. Her mouth moved; her throat constricted. Gerard heard her whisper, "T-Terryn?"

"Fight it," Terryn said. His voice was so rough, so wild, he did not sound like himself. "Fight it, Ayleth.

Please."

She moaned, and her head dropped back across his arm, the tall points of the Crown resting on the ground beneath her.

Ayleth lay curled up in darkness.

Her body burned, not with fire, but with magic far beyond anything she could bear. Not even the purifying flames of the Evanderians would destroy her like this. Those flames could only devour her body. This fire would devour her will and autonomy. Her self. Her very soul.

Oromor was everywhere, permeating her mind, penetrating deeper with every gasp of breath she managed to take between her screams. And there was nothing she could do to stop it.

Mistress!

Ayleth's soul quickened at the sound of that voice. So distant, so desperate, but true.

Mistress! Mistress!

"*Laranta?*" She whispered the name, her spirit

trembling with the effort required. Soon even this would be taken from her. Oromor would not allow another shade to dwell within this body. She could feel how it plunged its shadowy fingers deeper into her mind and memories, digging down toward her spirit core where Laranta was anchored. When it found that anchor, Oromor would rip it out and send Laranta hurtling forth to be swallowed by the Haunts.

And Ayleth's soul? It would neither ascend to the Goddess's light nor fall into the eternal damnation of the Haunts. No. Her doom was as Odile predicted—she would be devoured by Oromor. Still existing, still present, but utterly consumed.

Though her ravaged mind protested, Ayleth braced her remaining will and forced a projected image to take shape. It was thin, colorless, almost transparent, a mere specter of herself. But it was *her.* Using this projected form to steady her spirit, she rose and faced the churning darkness surrounding her.

Oromor was everywhere. Oromor was everything. What a fool she was to think she could fight this power! What a fool she was to think there would be any hope for freedom. There was no hope, no help, no—

Mistress!

"*Laranta,*" Ayleth whispered again. Then she wrapped her arms around her middle and sank down into a small huddled ball. As she curled up, she plunged, sending her awareness down through the layers of her possessed mind, falling through the darkness, through memories and dreams both remembered and forgotten. Down through every emotion of loyalty, betrayal, despair. She plummeted farther and farther, faster and faster.

Oromor felt her descent. She sensed its awareness focusing in on her. It streaked after her, pursuing no more than a breath in her wake.

She tumbled out at last onto a stony, uneven surface, like the floor of a deep cavern in the center of the world. Her projected image sprawled flat, the breath knocked out of her. But she pushed up at once, blinking hard against the brilliant light streaming into her eyes.

Directly in front of her, no more than an arm's stretch away, floated a perfect orb that shone like a small sun. She knew what it was, though she had never in all her mental wanderings penetrated so deeply inside herself before. It was the core of her soul, the very center of her being.

And anchored fast to that core was the soul tether binding Laranta to her.

Laranta appeared on the far side of the orb. At first, she was nothing but spirit, formless and strange. But she swiftly solidified into the familiar wolf shape Ayleth knew so well. *Mistress!* she barked and lunged forward.

"*Laranta.*" Ayleth scrambled up, her transparent image shivering and unsteady. She had moments before Oromor would arrive. Less than moments, for this was a place outside of time, so nothing could truly be measured by it. In reality, Oromor had already found her, had always found her, had long ago destroyed her. This battle was lost before it began. But in this tiny fraction of eternity, her mind told her she had precious seconds to spare. Seconds to leap across the little space separating her from her shade, to throw her arms around that shaggy black neck.

"*Laranta, Laranta,*" she crooned, pressing her face into midnight fur and breathing in the wolf shade's wildness. "*I'm sorry. We can't escape. It will find us, and it will tear us apart. But we won't be separated, Laranta. I swear it! We'll go together to the Haunts if I can only—"*

Laranta pulled her huge head back, looked Ayleth in the eyes. She opened her mouth as though to speak.

But Oromor was there.

Darkness more profound than doom, overwhelming, all-consuming, surrounded the flickering spirit-orb, blotting out its flickering light. Ayleth screamed. Far away, her body screamed as well, writhing in agonies inexpressible as the crown burned into her head, sending ribbons of red flame shooting across her body.

Laranta threw back her head and howled. For another precious, life-encompassing instant, Ayleth felt solid wolf-substance wrapped tight in her arms. It was already fading, slipping away, their mental projections vanishing as Ayleth's mind gave in to Oromor's relentless and inexorable power.

Then, suddenly, Ayleth found herself gazing into a pair of glowing eyes. Laranta's eyes, full of life. Full of spirit. Ayleth tried to speak. But she couldn't. Words and reason were stripped away. Her wolf shade bared shining sharp teeth.

Mistress, she said. *I love.*

The next moment she was gone.

The soul-orb flared bright, brighter than before. Bright enough to blind Ayleth's spirit-eyes, to blast her projected form to nothing. The pale little body she'd struggled to hold onto disintegrated, and Ayleth flew wildly into the darkness, away from the orb. With an effort of pure will, she pulled her awareness back into a concentrated center and gazed into the brilliance.

She saw two shadows moving, swirling around the orb. Two spirits—one, a being like a tall, thin woman, with elongated arms and massive, spider-like hands—the other, a wolf, wild and snarling. The woman shadow lashed out at the wolf, cutting into her, shredding her substance. The soul tether binding Laranta to the orb flared a raw, vicious red.

Laranta's teeth flashed in a ferocious smile. Then she lunged, taking her tether between her teeth.

Ayleth saw. She realized.

"*NO!*" she screamed, her voice swallowed up in Oromor's echoing roar of dismay.

With a single twist of her jaws, Laranta snapped the

soul tether in two.

A tremendous hurricane of spirit-storm erupted in that small space. The two dark souls whirled, caught in the maelstrom. But Ayleth remained apart, untouched, unable to reach them even when she threw herself forward, screaming and screaming. She watched in horror, unable to grasp what she saw. Her mind approached the very brink of madness.

She saw Laranta's jaws catch hold of the shadow-woman's thin neck. She felt the enormity of violently liberated shade power, far worse than any violent death she'd ever dealt. Oromor's shriek shattered the stone walls of that cavern and brought them crumbling down on all sides. The shadow-woman scrabbled at Laranta's head, tearing at her eyes, tearing at her spirit substance. But the funneling storm carried them up, up, up, away from the spirit-orb, away from Ayleth.

Ayleth felt the moment when Laranta burst free of her body, dragging Oromor with her. She felt the tear in reality as the Haunts opened to claim them. She felt the sudden cavernous emptiness in her soul.

She collapsed in a pool of shadowy nothingness,

unable to project a form, unable to think, unable to feel. Unable to bear her own existence.

For the first time in her life, she was alone.

CHAPTER 21

THE SHOCK OF MAGIC WAS SO GREAT, IT KNOCKED AYLETH out of Terryn's arms and sent him hurtling back against a finger pillar. He struck his head, and his vision danced. Nisirdi's wings flared bright on either side of him, trying to close around his soul, trying to protect him. The idol swayed again, and a deep groan issued from down below.

Terryn struggled up and peered out between his shade's shining wings, searching for Ayleth. She lay in the center of the palm with her limbs outspread, her back arched at an extreme angle, as though her spine would break. The crown gripped her head crushingly tight, and red light glared out from its living metal, from her skin, from her eyes. It was so bright that everything else seemed like utter darkness by comparison. Yet it wasn't a light that illuminated. Instead, it devoured.

The crown burned into her skull, and her scream was endless, unbroken even by a gasp for breath. In the ether above her, a strange tumult stirred and then broke into a storm of spirit-stuff that Terryn's mortal eyes could not bear to look upon. He blinked into shadow vision and saw, or thought he saw, the dark shape of a wolf leap out from Ayleth's breast, dragging with it something that clung to the crown with many finger-like protrusions. Something like a long, lean woman, but bizarrely exaggerated in form, with a neck as long as an arm, and a spear-wedge head, and hair like forked serpents' tongues. The woman fought with the wolf, clinging to the crown, but the wolf was empowered by a force of energy like that created by a violent death, only far greater.

Overhead, above the fingers of the idol hand, the Haunts opened. The horror of that crushing realm fell like hail and brimstone down upon them. The woman-like spirit shrieked, its voice slicing Terryn's spirit even as Ayleth's unending scream tore at his heart. Terryn wanted to hide his face, but he made himself look closer, made himself search for the mortal-soul orb in that confusion of spirits. But the tangle of the two shades, wolf and woman, was too wild, too exaggerated, too frenetic for him to discern anything in their midst.

"*Nisirdi!*" he cried, reaching along the soul tether for his light-dragon. "*Nisirdi, help them!*"

I cannot help this time, his shade responded, its voice ringing like clear bells through the hellish chorus of sounds. *I cannot reach them. Not now.*

The Haunts yawned wider, sucking viciously at the mortal world. The red *oblivis* in the air whirled up into its home in a maelstrom of malicious poison. The vortex gripped at the wolf shade, dragging it out in a stream of darkness so that the body dissipated to almost nothing, and only the head remained, clinging to that long woman. For a second, Terryn thought the wolf would lose its grip.

Then, with a last wild twist of its entire being, it wrenched the other shade loose from the crown. A roaring burst blasted Terryn, pressing him flat against the pillar, and only Nisirdi's wings wrapped around his soul protected him from greater harm. Noises like the antithesis to all music reverberated through the ether, striking blow after blow at his soul, and Nisirdi's wings shivered, their light pulsing in response to each hit.

It seemed an age . . . but at last the Haunts closed. The assault ended. Terryn pushed back Nisirdi's wings, his eyes dazzled and half blinded. He blinked many times before his vision cleared enough for him to see anything in the mortal world.

Faint starlight filtered down from on high, illuminating the curves of the idol's hands, the ragged edges of the broken finger, the heap of bones and blood that was Odile's corpse, and the shaking figure of Gerard crouched in the shadows near the thumb.

Terryn's gaze fixed on Ayleth lying still in the center of the palm. So still, she must be dead.

With a strangled cry, he crawled across the oblidite to reach her, catching hold of her arm and pulling her into his lap. Her skin smoked, and her hair and much of her clothing was burned away. But the burns on her skin were not as bad as he would have thought, only raw and red and a little blistered in places. He carefully lifted her head and shoulders in his arms and pushed the crown off her brow.

It fell with a dull ringing thud and rolled several feet away before coming to a stop. The *eitr* was dull and dead, all the strange living force gone out of it. Its tines bent and broke on impact with the much harder oblidite.

Terryn pulled his gaze away from that evil sight, looking down into Ayleth's face. Her eyes were partially open and dull, her blistered lips sagging open. He pressed her to his chest, smearing blood from Fendrel's cuts onto her face and neck. Hands shaking, he pressed his fingers to her pulse. To his shock, he found a heartbeat. He blinked into shadow sight again, Nisirdi's light gleaming in his eyes, and gazed down inside her.

There, deep in her center, he saw the glow of her soul, present and strong. But there was no trace of any shade spirit. Neither Elemental nor Feral.

He drew a ragged breath and crushed her face against his chest again. She was alive. A miracle beyond anything he could have hoped for. Alive and breathing and whole.

What her mind would be when she woke, he couldn't imagine. For now, he didn't care. He clung to her, pressing his lips against her burned scalp again and again. Never again, never, never would he stop himself from kissing her; never again would he hold himself back. Not while he had breath in his body.

Nisirdi's head appeared at his shoulder, great orb eyes blinking in wonder. *I have never seen it done before.*

"*What?*" Terryn asked in his mind even as his mouth continued to kiss Ayleth's head. "*What haven't you seen?*"

A shade that would willingly break the soul tether binding her to her host. She could have used the violence of the break to escape the Haunts . . . but instead, she channeled all that violent power into tearing Oromor free of the eitr *crown.* The light-dragon solemnly shook its elegant head. *It is a wonder, Terryn du Balafre. Even now, even after all these ages, the power of love can still dazzle my gaze.*

Terryn looked at his shade, unable to fathom the words still ringing in his ears. He would store them away in his mind, analyze them later, and decide what they meant. Not now. Now, he simply sat there, holding Ayleth.

Movement caught Terryn's eye, and he looked up sharply. His face tensed, then relaxed, going almost completely slack, unable to find the strength to express the relief he felt at the sight of Gerard. His brother was cut and bruised and battered, his neck a mass of ugly wounds where he'd been strung up by the *oblivis* noose. But he was alive and standing on his own two feet.

Gerard approached slowly, placing each foot with care. "Terryn," he said after three paces. Then he stopped, and though his mouth remained open, no other sound followed. Terryn couldn't answer, so they simply gazed at one another, their spirits momentarily suspended in a moment of true gladness mingled with pain.

Suddenly, Ayleth shuddered in Terryn's arms.

"Ayleth?" He loosened his hold on her, let her pull away from his chest, let her head roll back into the crook of his arm. Her body jolted again, as though a burst of energy rolled up through her spine. One arm flailed weakly, and her hand grasped desperately at thin air.

A horrible choking sound clogged her throat, and Terryn was just fast enough to sit her up so that she vomited to the side rather than all over him and herself.

He held her tenderly until the heaving passed. She sagged back into his arms and weakly wiped the back of her hand across her mouth. Her body trembled violently, as though she would fly to pieces.

She turned her head and looked up at him. For an instant, he could not see the burns, couldn't see the brokenness, couldn't see the blisters on her lips, the smears of *oblivis* streaking her face. He couldn't see the horrible blackened band across her bald head. He saw only the sudden joy flooding her face. And she was so beautiful.

But the moment passed. Her eyes widened, and she clutched at her chest with both hands. "Laranta," she gasped.

Then she threw back her head and howled. "Laranta! *Laranta!*" She pounded her chest, pounded at her heart, then her fingers moved to tear at her head, and she screamed that name again and again both in her physical voice and in her spirit voice, which scraped against Terryn's ascendant shadow senses. "Laranta! *No, no, no!*"

She crumpled up into a little ball of nothing, weeping even as her soul kept screaming. And Terryn could do nothing but hold her close as Nisirdi wrapped diaphanous wings around them both.

Gerard turned his back to Terryn and Ayleth, unable to bear the sight of so much pain, so much suffering. He wasn't part of it in any case. Something was going on there, something in a realm he could almost sense but couldn't see. Something dark and terrible. And private.

So, he turned away, breathing hard and trying his best not to hear the gut-wrenching sounds Ayleth made. She was alive at least. The vision Nilly gave him—it had shown nothing beyond the swing of his sword. He'd assumed he would die when the blow struck; he'd assumed he and she would destroy each other. And the world would be made a better, safer place.

Yet here they were. Alive, if not entirely whole.

And the world . . . would it ever again be safe?

Darkness caught his eye, a deeper darkness against the smooth oblidite of the idol's hand. He took a few steps and bent to pick up the *eitr* crown. It was strangely light and bitterly cold. One touch, and he knew that it was dead. His fingers closing around one sharply pointed tine, he turned and carried it several paces across the hand.

He came to a halt over the head of Odile.

Blood still drained from her crumpled body a few feet away. The head lay in a dark pool, the face rolled up toward him, the dead eyes staring straight at him. Looking down into that face, Gerard saw Ayleth again as he had seen her in his vision, as he had seen her but a few moments ago. The memory twisted in his breast and he felt . . . he felt . . .

He laid his free hand over his heart. Was this feeling compassion? Sorrow? It seemed unbelievable. But also undeniable. He gazed into that dead face and wondered suddenly who this person was. This person who had become Dread Odile, who had become the Poison of Perrinion. He wondered if there had ever been a time when he and she could have spoken to one another as equals, as friends. If there was ever a time when they needn't have been enemies.

For what had been Dread Odile's ultimate hope for this world? To establish her city as a safe haven for shade-taken in a world that hunted them down.

His knees shook. Gerard surrendered to the impulse that seized him and knelt before Odile, setting the crown off to one side. His mouth was dry when he opened it, and Ayleth's despairing howls rang out behind him, echoing against the idol's fingers. The idol swayed again, and his stomach plunged with the certain knowledge that the whole thing would soon fall. But for the moment, he remained where he was.

"I will do it," he whispered, looking into those dead eyes. "I will establish the safe haven, Odile. My father was your enemy. But if you can see me from wherever your spirit now resides, know this: I am and will always be a friend to your people. I will establish in Perrinion a home for the shade-taken, and I will drive out the Order of Evander. It may take years. It may take my entire life. But I will see the hand of peace extended, ready to be grasped by those who will respond in kind. There will be brotherhood between mortals and shades."

He reached out, his hand flinching a little, and closed the dead woman's eyes. *"May the Mother receive you who hath called you,"* he whispered, *"and may the heavenly spirits conduct you to the Gates of Light."*

When he lifted his hand, Odile's head and body disintegrated into a cloud of *oblivis* and drifted away through the fingers of the idol. Gerard watched, and his eyes widened as he saw a greater cloud rising beyond the idol. It billowed upward, so thick that it blocked out the stars, like the oncoming mass of a huge thunderstorm. But a breeze blew, soft and sweet, and all the *oblivis* dissipated in a mass of glitter, and then . . . nothing.

Gerard rose to his feet and staggered to the space between the idol's finger and thumb. He gazed out, and his jaw dropped. The Witchwood was gone. The endless acres where that forest once stretched now lay bare beneath the starlit sky.

Below, in the ruined streets of Dulimurian, figures moved. Even from so high above, Gerard believed he saw the bright red of Evanderian hoods.

He turned around. "Terryn," he spoke softly.

Terryn, holding Ayleth as she wailed against his chest, looked up and met his gaze. His face was desperate and strained.

"It's time to go, Terryn," Gerard said.

CHAPTER 22

CERINE LIMPED SOFT-FOOTED DOWN THE DARKENED halls of Dunloch, the lantern she carried creating a small sphere of light around her. She shouldn't be on her feet with her ankle still throbbing so painfully, but she couldn't rest. Not tonight. Possibly never again.

She stopped at the door to her own chambers and peeked into the room. She'd put both Nilly and Ducette in her bed to sleep, and the two of them now curled up among her pillows like a pair of cats. Since she couldn't sense the spirits indwelling them, she couldn't tell whether they rested as well. At least their exhausted bodies would know some peace.

Pulling the door softly shut, she continued along the passage to the gallery above the Great Hall, where she peered down to the floor below. The guards on either side of the main doors slumped at their stations, possibly asleep on their feet. The entire household of Dunloch was still, shade-taken and untaken alike. She might be the only one awake in the whole castle.

Turning away from the Great Hall, she made for the door leading to the northeast tower, climbed the winding stair, and stepped out into a bitter-cold night beneath a blanket of stars. The wind blew hard, but she walked up to the stone crenellations and set her lantern there. Just in case someone might see it. Just in case someone needed a gleam of hope in the darkness.

In her left hand she clutched Gerard's letter, her knuckles white from squeezing it so hard. All day she had carried it with her, telling herself she would open it soon. But she couldn't bring herself to read it . . . not when it would most likely contain the last words she ever heard from Gerard.

Now, she stepped closer to the lantern and lifted the letter. After swallowing hard and setting her jaw, as though steeling herself for the torturer's knife, she broke the seal and unfolded the crumpled paper. Her frightened eyes quickly skimmed over the words.

Three words.

Only three.

No signature. But none was needed. Cerine knew that hand too well to mistake it for any other.

She read that brief line, which expressed so much so simply. And she read it again and again, drinking it in. Words he had tried to express to her in person but which she had refused to believe.

Did she believe him now? Would she accept his final confession?

She dragged in a breath, crumpled the paper in her hands, and stared over the battlements into the night. For the moment, she could not think, could not see, could not feel the biting wind in her face. There was room in her awareness only for those words and for her own vicious regrets.

Suddenly, she frowned.

Something was different about the darkness. Something about that far horizon. Was she imagining things now? Did she imagine that massive cloud rising into the sky, glittering—not with reflected light but with its own otherworldly glow—and then vanishing to nothing?

She let out a gust of breath she hadn't realized she was holding and dragged in a gasp of air. Something was different. Something had changed—as if a massive burden had been lifted, a gross sin inexplicably expunged.

The Witchwood was gone.

At dawn, five riders set out from Dunloch, racing into the rising sun. They led extra horses and carried the supplies Cerine had hastily packed—food and water and medicinal items.

She wished she dared send more people but couldn't risk them, having no idea what these five brave men rode into. She might well have sent them into an onslaught of witches and monsters.

They had left with promises to return as soon as possible, bringing back word of their findings. Now she must wait. Again.

Cerine kept watch from the tower. Occasionally someone would come up the stairs, one of her Siveline Sisters or a member of the castle staff bringing her food or drink and begging her to come down and rest. But although she agreed to having a chair brought up so that she might sit, she couldn't bear to leave the tower. All day she maintained her lookout role.

The sun set at last. And still there was no word. The riders did not return.

Cerine lit her lantern and wrapped the thick robes someone had draped over her shoulders tight around her body. Fingers plucked at her sleeve, and a distant, pestering voice begged her to come inside, to sleep, to at least put her head down a spell. She ignored them.

The night deepened. A chill crept through her, into her heart. She heard voices rising from the open chapel windows below—the Siveline Sisters gathered to sing prayers and petitions. Perhaps she should join them. Perhaps, even after all this time, the Goddess might still hear them.

Or perhaps Cerine was a deluded fool.

Darkness deepened around her, and the stars above seemed to retreat to a cold distance where their light could offer no comfort. If anything, their presence made the night seem darker still. Was that all Cerine's prayers were? Pitiful sparks of light that served only to deepen the horrors of the world around her? Did she really believe that her quavering voice, the wordless groans of her spirit, could move the compassion of a great and distant Goddess?

Why should the Goddess care for her? For Gerard, for any of them? If She was indeed deity, why should She trouble Herself with the small doings of mortals? Their little histories, their little kingdoms rising and falling and crashing, all contained within the finite and infinitesimal boundaries of Time. No, no. If She was Divine, then the tremulous prayers uttered by mortal lips and mortal hearts could never hope to reach Her in Her high heaven.

Why? Why, why? The darkness seemed to echo down at Cerine in a booming sort of silence, a voice she could not ignore. Why did she cling to her belief like some foolish child? Why did she not give it up now and face the realities of this world? This cruel world where prophecies were manipulated by cruel men. Where destinies were decided and dictated by those with the power to enforce them. Where all that was good and holy was eventually crushed beneath the heel of all that was base and ugly. A world in which she could hardly bear to live.

"Goddess," Cerine whispered.

The silence terrified her. It echoed within the chambers of her doubting heart.

"Goddess . . ." she whispered again.

She could say no more. If that prayer alone—that small, desperate prayer—wasn't enough, no chants sung in multiple verses by a choir of hundreds could hope to penetrate the sky.

She waited in a frozen, timeless moment. A moment more agonizing than any other moment of her existence. A moment in which she knew she would rise or fall; she would live or die. An eternity of hell contained in a single fraction of time and space.

Then.

Through the silence.

Through the shimmer of frozen starlight.

In the depths of her own fear-filled heart, in the darkest chamber, a soft whisper . . .

Beloved.

A heralding trumpet sounded in the night, bright notes breaking the silence like fireworks erupting in fountains of gold. Cerine whirled from her study of the eastern horizon, turning her eyes instead to the southwest, toward the gate, the single entrance into Dunloch across the bridge. The trumpet sounded again. She recognized the song it played, those seven notes blasted in quick succession. It was the herald song of the king.

"Gerard?" she whispered.

The next moment, she was in motion. Leaving her lantern behind, Cerine raced down the tower stairs in the dark as fast as she could on her injured ankle, but she was so slow! So slow! It felt like a dream, that sluggish sensation of sticky air holding her back when she wanted to run faster, harder. She tripped on the last steps and fell headlong out of the stairwell and into the passage at the tower's base, catching herself with her hands. Pain shot through one wrist now as well as her leg, and she bit down hard on a curse even as she regained her feet and hastened along the corridor, using the wall for support. On every side, doors were opening, voices murmuring, and guards' boots clattered on marble tiles.

She gained the top of the grand staircase and, leaning heavily against the banister, half tumbled down to the main floor. The slumbering men on watch had awakened and opened the doors. They now peered out, their pikes held at aggressive angles.

"Make way!" Cerine cried. They parted at once, giving her space to limp between them and stand on the porch, gazing out across the courtyard.

Down the center of the drive trotted the horses she had sent out an eternity ago. Her five riders and . . . and more. Riding the extra horses. She didn't see how many, for the torchlight flared sudden and bright, illuminating the face of the man riding in the vanguard.

On trembling legs, Cerine staggered down the steps, but at their base she stopped short, suddenly afraid. What if she woke up now? What if this was a dream, and when she opened her eyes and lifted her head from her pillow, he wasn't there?

But then he saw her.

Gerard spurred his horse into a gallop, leaving the white drive to ride straight across the winter-dead lawn. He was battered, bloody, dirty, and disgusting like she'd never seen him before. Ugly red wounds scored his face, and horrible bruises ringed his neck. Surely, she couldn't dream him in such detail.

She threw herself at him just as he leaped down from his horse and caught her in his arms. The kiss he pressed to her mouth was awkward, almost painful, and he had to adjust his hold on her, adjust his position to give her another, gentler kiss, which lasted longer than the first. Tears streamed down her face, and her whole body shook. But he didn't melt away in her arms. She held him fast, held him as though she would never let go.

But then he pulled back. It was a kind of agony to feel his lips leave hers, but a relief to gaze up into his eyes. They stared at one another. She didn't wait for him to speak, didn't wait for any explanations.

"I love you," she gasped. "I love—" She couldn't finish, cut off by another kiss.

This time when he lifted his head, his arms still wrapped tightly around her, Gerard managed to speak. "Be my wife, Cerine." His voice was thick, rough, and urgent. "I beg you."

She managed to nod, and then she was kissing him again even as the air around her filled with the sound of hooves and many voices speaking and all the tumult of the king's triumphant return.

CHAPTER 23

AYLETH WALKED IN THE PINE FOREST OF HER MIND.

It was still. So silent. So empty.

Her bare feet crunched on the prickly red carpet of pine straw, deftly avoiding any sharp-edged pinecones or protruding roots. Pale light streamed through the green boughs, patterning her shadowed path in spots of white, and she breathed deep of the perfumes of the forest, so intense that they felt real even though she knew this was only a dream.

For days she had run frantically, tearing through the deep forest paths, up and down the inclines from the highest crests to the lowest valleys. Her voice had echoed across the heavy sky, calling, screaming, and crying with no hope of a reply. She'd known the hunt was futile. She had hunted, nonetheless.

That hunt was over. Now she simply walked. Listening to the silence in her head that echoed on and on and on. Sometimes she reached for a soul tether that was no longer there, feeling the emptiness where it ought to be, like an amputee scratching at a phantom limb.

How long had she wandered? Days? Weeks? Minutes? It didn't matter. She was unconscious, and her physical body lay somewhere far away, vulnerable. Now and then she heard voices murmuring through the atmosphere of gray overhead, but never loud enough that she could understand what they said. Perhaps she simply didn't want to understand.

They'd probably drugged her. Given her something to calm her, body and soul. Something to make her stop running and running and running through her mind. It was probably the drug that had slowed her to this sedate pace, forced her into this calmness. She felt panic simmering just below the surface, down beneath the straw-strewn ground. But it was fading now, giving place to this calm and to . . . heaviness.

What drug had they used? she wondered idly. Not *sòm*. *Sòm* was meant to suppress shades. She didn't need *sòm*. Not anymore.

How tired she was! Yet she kept on walking, resisting the urge to sit, to rest. The trees thinned around her, opening at last to a clear space. She stepped from the pine shadows onto the rocky ledge of a deep gorge and recognized it at once—the site of her hidden memories.

But those memories were no longer hidden. She could feel them, alive and active in the forest around her. The drug kept them silent and distant, but while standing here on the edge of the gorge, she felt them closer than before. Perhaps the sedative was starting to wear off.

Something approached along the gorge's lip, off to her right. Ayleth didn't turn to face the tall, slim figure as it drew up beside her. They stood together, gazing at that view, that break in the surface of her mind world, that plunging crevice into deeper parts of her soul. It was breathtaking, surrounded by the rises and valleys of the dense forest beneath that gauzy gray sky.

If she were to reach out, she could touch her companion. But it would vanish like mist if she did, for it was only a memory. Not real.

The tall woman spoke at last. Her voice was as dark as night. *"I would have loved you if only you had let me."*

Ayleth didn't answer. She waited, and the memory finally turned and walked away again, leaving her alone at the gorge. A wind howled up from below, blowing against her bare skin and her long, flowing hair. It was a cold blast that cut through flesh straight to the bone. She sucked in a sharp breath and closed her eyes, embracing the sting.

Something called to her on that wind. A voice she didn't know but almost recognized. A voice from among those newly reclaimed memories sighing, *Come home . . . Come home . . . Come home . . .*

Ayleth woke to another blast of cold air, real and sharp against her physical body.

Her eyes flew open, and for a dizzying moment she thought she was back home in Gillanluòc. She gazed up at the rafters of a circular tower ceiling, noting places where the thatch had fallen and light crept through. She felt the heat of warmed chimney stones at her back, and it was all so familiar she could half believe, half pretend she was just a girl again, a young apprentice venatrix waking up in her familiar room, facing a familiar day—a routine of poison studies and weapons practice and histories and horses and recitation and demonstration.

But within the first blink, that little fantasy melted away. She was not a child. This was not Gillanluòc, not her bed. The placement of the window in the room was off, the set of the rafters similar but not the same.

Laranta was gone. She was alone. This was the new reality of her existence.

Ayleth blinked a second time, more slowly than the last. When her eyelashes lifted, she peered around the room. It was familiar to her, though not as familiar as her room at Gillanluòc. This must be Milisendis. She saw her few belongings arranged more neatly than she had left them—her garments folded and stacked on a spindly chair, her boots standing tall by the door. She lay on a bed, which surprised her. There hadn't been a bed in this room before, only a straw mattress and a pile of blankets.

The rug tacked up over the window slit had fallen, letting the icy blast of wind through. Snow piled in small drifts on the floor, and the air bit at her skin—a shock, yet also a relief. Painful though it might be, it provided a sensation to focus on other than the aching emptiness inside.

Ayleth sat up, shivering, and hugged herself tight. She seemed to have kicked off a stack of woolen blankets, and the bricks someone placed at the foot of her bed had gone cold. She wore only a linen shift and . . . She put her hand up, feeling the folds of the scarf wrapped around her head. With a single tug, she pulled it free and ran her other hand across the stubble of her bare, scarred scalp. Strange—she'd never felt such cold on her head before. She'd never realized the natural warmth hair provided until it was gone.

Her fingers lingered on the tight, puckered scar ringing her brow.

Images flashed through her mind—images of that dark

spirit, that long woman reaching for her in the cavernous depths of her soul. Images of burning *oblivis,* and the crown clutching her fast. She felt the sickening sensation in her gut of the idol swaying underfoot, of a sword swinging at her neck. Of blood, violence, chaos, and Laranta—

No.

She closed her eyes and bowed her shoulders, hunching against those visions. No, no. This time she was going to stay aware, stay in the present moment. She wasn't going to lose herself in madness and raving again.

A little table beside the bed hadn't been there before. It held an arrangement of bottles and glasses, some of them used. She picked up one bottle and gave it a shake, seeing how little of the dose was left. She wondered . . .

Footsteps sounded on the stair outside her door. Ayleth turned sharply, watchful. She knew that tread. She didn't need shadow senses to recognize it, to know who would soon appear in the doorway.

The latch turned. The hinges creaked. Hollis peered into the room. Her gaze moved from Ayleth to the pile of blankets on the floor to the open window and the snow.

Frowning, she stepped across the room and took up the fallen window-rug, tacking it firmly back in place. The room darkened, and Ayleth reflexively tried to blink into shadow sight to compensate. But nothing happened. Nothing but a painful jolt of remembrance.

Hollis turned to Ayleth, and the two of them faced each other in the dimness. A long silence followed.

"You probably have a lot of questions," Hollis said at length.

Ayleth didn't respond.

Hollis stepped across the room and bent to retrieve the fallen blankets and scarf. She gently wrapped the blankets around Ayleth, tucking them under her legs to protect her bare skin from the cold. Just like a mother should do.

"It's been fourteen days," she continued, her voice not at all maternal. She used the abrupt venatrix voice Ayleth knew so well. "The king—Gerard du Glaive—is alive and restored to Dunloch. He is gathering men from surrounding boroughs and will soon make the journey to Telianor, where he will lay claim to his father's crown." Hollis stepped back and began to fold the headscarf slowly and precisely. "I will ride with him. I, and Terryn du Balafre and Kephan du Tam. A few others from Breçar as well. It is hoped that you will join the procession."

She laid the scarf in Ayleth's lap, then quickly turned and crossed the room. After shifting the folded garments off the spindly chair, she took a seat, perched very upright with her hands on her knees, as though she were making a report. "I don't know how aware you have been these last two weeks," she said. "We have spoken to you many times, and sometimes you seemed to hear, but others . . ." She shook her head. "I will tell you what I can. Feel free to stop me and ask questions as you need."

She began to talk, filling the cold air with her words. She spoke of the Witchwood—gone. Of the *eitr* crown—dead, no longer possessed. She spoke of the idol—fallen three days after the events that took place in the palm of its upraised hand. She spoke of the death and loss of many, including Fendrel du Glaive. She spoke of the king's return to Dunloch and even of the shade-taken currently residing in his household under his royal protection.

"These are uncertain times," she said. "Changes are afoot across the land, which is to be expected with the rise of a new king. But I anticipate a peaceful transfer of power at Telianor. At first. Eventually some of the king's new ideas are sure to . . . cause a stir. There may be war. With the castras. With the other Gaulian kingdoms." She shook her head, one eyebrow raised, but her expression otherwise calm. "Who can know the future? Even Seers see no more than shadows."

Throughout her talk, Ayleth held her tongue. She had no questions and felt only relief when Hollis finally ran out of words.

At last Hollis rose. She took the stack of garments and placed them on Ayleth's bed, then moved the boots by the door closer as well. "If you feel up to it, rise, dress, and come downstairs. If not, I will return in an hour with food."

With those words, she left. Ayleth sat for some while. Then, slowly, she reached out and plucked her quilted trousers from the top of the garment pile. Something fell out and landed in thick folds on the floor, drawing her eye. A bright splash of red fabric. Her hood.

The horse standing in Chestibor's stall wasn't Chestibor. It was some liver-colored mare with a flaxen mane, a beast Ayleth didn't recognize. The only other horse in the stable was Hollis's own gray, so she guessed the mare was intended to be her mount. Frowning, she went about finding tack and saddled up. Despite all the aches and pains in her body, it felt good to be doing the familiar task, motions her muscles managed with no thought.

She was securing her travel bags to the saddle when Hollis appeared in the stable doorway. "Ayleth," she said and nothing more.

Ayleth cast her a glance before returning her focus to her task. She fastened the last of the buckles and knotted the last of the leather ties. Then, taking up the horse's reins, she led it out of its stall and down the central aisle of the small stable.

Hollis stepped aside, giving her room to pass into the outpost yard. "Ayleth," she said again as Ayleth paused to check the girth and stirrups. "Where are you going?"

"Home," Ayleth answered.

"Home? What do you mean? Are you . . . Do you mean Gillanluòc?"

Ayleth looked over her shoulder, fixing Hollis with a cold stare. "I'm going home," she said. "The only home that has ever been mine. The home you took from me when you killed my mother and my brothers and sisters."

Hollis went very pale, and her eyes stood out bright and sharp beneath her drawn brows. "Ayleth—" she began.

Ayleth cut her off. "What do you think has happened, Hollis? What do you think there is between us? Do you imagine I'm still that girl who sat at your knee, who hung on your every word? The girl you molded and shaped with your lies and your half-truths? Do you think I'm *your* daughter?"

She might as well have struck her former mistress a blow to the gut. Hollis took a step back, her shoulders bowing slightly. Ayleth had never seen such an expression of pain in her eyes. "I did what I had to do," she said. "Your mother . . . she was a murderer. Worse than a murderer. You don't know Olecia di Mauvalis; you don't know who or what she was. She delighted in the deaths of mortals, she toyed with them and tortured them and—"

"You are a *liar,*" Ayleth breathed. She'd intended to scream, but the words came out a whisper. "You have always been a liar. You've manipulated me from the start. This, even this . . . more manipulation. More lies. Or perhaps it is the truth? How would I know?"

Her horse shivered and pranced in place, agitated by the malicious tension it sensed in the air. Ayleth stroked the mare's neck. When she spoke again, her voice was calmer, clearer. "There's no point to it anymore. I've done what you wanted. I've killed Dread Odile. I've served my purpose. And now I'm done."

Hollis took a step toward her, one hand outstretched. "I did what I had to do," she said softly. "I know you don't understand. But I swear, I did what I did to save you. To protect you. I . . . I gave you everything I knew to give. I know I made mistakes—"

Ayleth recoiled from her hand. "Mistakes?" She nearly choked on the word. "Is that what you call slaughtering my family? A mistake? Is that what you call stripping my mind of all memory of them?" She braced herself, then took a step toward Hollis, who hastily retracted her hand

and backed away. "You took them from me. *You took them from me.*"

The urge for death, for violence, roared in her head. As though Laranta were still there, still present, still driving her with Feral instincts. Ayleth turned away quickly. If she looked into Hollis's face one moment more, she would try to kill her. How she would manage it without Laranta's strength, she couldn't say. But she would try. And she would regret it.

So, she turned away before the impulse became too great to control. Her breath frosted the air before her face. She was suddenly weak, dizzy, uncertain she could find the strength to mount the horse. But she couldn't stay here. Not for another minute.

Setting her boot to the stirrup, she gripped the saddle and swung herself up. When darkness filled her head, she caught hold of a handful of pale mane and managed to keep her seat until her vision cleared. Her right foot found the other stirrup, and she nudged the horse toward the gate, which stood open for her departure.

Hollis walked beside her at the horse's shoulder, breathing hard. "Ayleth," she said, "please. Don't leave like this. Please, Ayleth, you must believe me. If I could go back and make changes, I would. I love you. My dearest, my wild girl. You must know that I love you!"

"I would have loved you if only you had let me."

Ayleth pulled the red hood up over her bare head. Before her, the open road led up and out of the little stone valley in which Milisendis stood. She spurred the mare to a full gallop. The wind in her ears was almost enough to drown out Hollis's voice calling behind her:

"Ayleth! Ayleth, please!"

CHAPTER 24

"YOUR PARDON, VENATOR DU BALAFRE."

Terryn winced at the sound of the title. He was not a venator. Not anymore. But, after some argument, he had agreed to Gerard's request that he maintain the title with all its pretexts and implications for the time being, until the crown was secure, the ministers of the court appointed, and the kingdom once more firmly established following the loss of its king. It was a ruse Terryn disliked, but one he would be obliged to play for the next several years at least.

Soon enough, the castras would learn the truth. Soon enough, the heresies would come to light, and war would break out. A war as vicious as the Witch Wars unless he was much mistaken. Soon . . . not yet, but soon . . .

He'd set up an office for himself in the west-wing parlor, and he and Kephan had kept busy over the last two weeks, mostly managing the newly shade-taken denizens of Dunloch, teaching them to balance their possessing souls and control their powers. At times they resorted to Evanderian methods of suppression for the safety of the individual. But Terryn hoped, with time, to teach all of them to find a more harmonious mode of living. Success would depend greatly on both the individual human and shade in question.

When they weren't occupied with training, they shared the task of composing letters to various members of the castras across Gaulia and to certain of the more remote outposts. There were those, Kephan believed, who would ride to the king's banner if the right word could reach their ears at the right moment. Apparently, heresy had been brewing in the ranks for longer than Terryn realized.

The thought was unsettling yet, at the moment, encouraging as well.

Now Terryn looked up from the letter he was composing to see a young messenger boy in the doorway. "Yes, Billin?" he asked, setting aside his quill. At the edge of his vision, he saw Nisirdi lift its narrow, draconian head from where it had apparently been resting on a velvet lounge. This was a mere projection of his mind, but Terryn had become strangely used to seeing his light-dragon manifest in the room beside him even when he did not directly access its powers.

The boy, though untaken, cast a nervous sideways glance toward that part of the room, as though he somehow sensed the otherworldly presence. He chewed nervously on the inside of his cheek before saying quickly, "Your pardon, Venator, but . . . word's come from the stables. Venatrix di Ferosa arrived, looking for her horse. You left word that you were to be alerted if—"

Terryn was on his feet already. "Thank you, Billin," he said as he rushed out the door, leaving his letter and documents behind. Nisirdi rose and flowed through the air behind him, silent but ever near.

His heart thudding painfully, Terryn made his way to a back stair and charged down. He had protested at first when Hollis proposed taking Ayleth to Milisendis Outpost. He'd wanted to bring her back to Dunloch where he could keep an eye on her while simultaneously keeping an eye on Gerard. But Hollis was right—Ayleth would recover better in more familiar surroundings. The luxuries of the castle would only add to her stress. So, Hollis got her way and stayed on at Milisendis as Ayleth's nurse.

Terryn had ventured out there as often as possible. During the last fortnight, he'd ridden three times to the outpost and spent those days and nights at Ayleth's side as she slept or as she raved. He couldn't be certain she was aware of his presence, though sometimes he thought she might hear his voice, and he hoped it brought her comfort.

Every time he'd gone to visit, he'd thought of bringing Chestibor with him, knowing Ayleth would want to be reunited with her horse. But the thought had struck him—she would leave. When her reason finally returned to her, when she rose from her bed, she would pack up her belongings, mount her horse, and she would leave. And he would never see her again.

But if he kept Chestibor at Dunloch, she would have to come. Apparently, he'd been right. Once outside, he ran to the stable yard but saw no sign of a tall girl or her horse. He caught the elbow of the first stable boy that passed by. "Did a woman come?" he demanded. "Did she take a horse, a brown gelding away with her? A tall woman, and . . . and she'd have no hair."

"I don't know, sir," the boy said, shaking his head, his eyes round and frightened by the stern, scarred face glaring down at him. "There was a venatrix with a red hood. She may have been bald underneath, I couldn't say—"

"Where is she?"

"She's come and gone, sir. About a quarter of an hour—"

Terryn didn't wait to hear the rest. He rushed into the stable, shouting for someone to bring him a horse. In under five minutes he was mounted and riding across the bridge to the gate. The guards saw him coming and stepped aside to make room for him to pass. He slowed to shout, "Which way did the venatrix go?"

"North road," one of the men answered. Terryn wheeled his horse to the right and spurred it faster. Nisirdi flowed silently through the air behind him, following the tug of their connecting soul tether. After another ten minutes of hard riding, Terryn spied her ahead of him. He'd know that slim, upright figure even without the red hood pulled up over her head.

He shouted her name and saw her shoulders stiffen. She didn't turn to face him.

Cursing softly, Terryn leaned over his horse's neck and urged it faster. As he reached her side, he reined in sharply. His mount skidded on its heels, blowing and tossing its head angrily.

"Ayleth," Terryn said, his voice a sharp bark.

"Venator du Balafre," Ayleth answered quietly. She still didn't look at him. Her face, shadowed by her hood, remained fixed toward the horizon.

He studied her for some moments in silence. His visits to Milisendis, the long hours he'd sat by her bedside, had not helped him adjust to the sight of her without her shade. Looking at her with shadow sight was painful, like looking at an open wound that would never heal.

He blinked back into his mortal vision and studied at her profile instead. The sharp line of her jaw and the angles of her face had intensified following her ordeal. The hood covered her baldness, though he could see that dark stubble was growing in thick and would soon cover her scalp, her scars. The worst of the burns and blisters had already healed.

But her eyes . . . they were hollow. Haunted.

"Where are you going?" he demanded.

"Home," she said quietly. Still she did not turn.

He blinked, confused. "Where . . . where is your home?"

She drew a long breath and let it out in a longer sigh, the air puffing white from her lips. "The Skada Mountains," she said at last. "Somewhere. I'm not sure." Then she shrugged. "I'll know it when I find it."

"So . . . you're riding off into the wilderness. In winter. Alone?"

She nodded.

"You can't."

Only then did she look at him, her head turning

sharply in her hood. Her eyes flashed dangerously. "Watch me."

It was almost a relief to see that ferocity still present inside her. A relief to know that, though she had lost her shade, her magic, her unnatural powers, she had not lost her *self*. Ayleth was a force of nature all on her own. She had never needed a shade to strike terror into his heart.

He swallowed hard, his throat so swollen, he couldn't for the moment speak. Then he said, "What about Gerard?"

She didn't answer. She faced the road again, setting her chin a little higher than before, her jaw a little harder.

Terryn pressed on. "He needs you. He needs all of us. There will be difficult days ahead. Just now, the ministers of Telianor still believe him to be the rightful heir, but word will soon spread of the doings here in Wodechran Borough. There will be dissenters. And when it becomes public that he's protecting shade-taken, that he's brought an inborn child into his own household, the castras will rise up in protest. He will need all of us to support him if he is to keep his throne, and—"

"What a blessing it is that our Golden King has a

brother so loyal and true," Ayleth said. There was no malice in her words. They were spoken with perfect sincerity. "I'm confident that he will reign long and well so long as you are at his side."

Terryn's mouth hung open, and his hands pulled unconsciously at the reins, slowing his horse. She rode ahead several paces before he spurred his beast back into motion and maneuvered it in front of her gelding, cutting her off.

"I love you," he said.

She looked at him as though peering through a filmy veil. Then she dropped her gaze to her hands resting on the pommel of her saddle.

"I've loved you from the moment I first laid eyes on you," he continued. The words burned in his mouth, but he couldn't stop speaking. "I didn't realize what it was I felt then. I took one look at you, and it struck me at once like a spear to the heart: I knew that you would destroy me. I thought I hated you. Now I know better.

"You *have* destroyed me, Ayleth. Everything I thought I was. Everything I thought I would become. It's all ruined, shattered. Gone. And I couldn't be more grateful.

I couldn't be happier that the Goddess brought you and your destructive influence into my heart, turned you loose on my life to wreak your havoc. Because of what you've done to me, I can now be rebuilt into something new. Something better."

He turned his horse's head and moved the beast alongside Chestibor, close enough that, if he had the courage, he could reach out and take her hand. But he couldn't quite make himself do it. His hand froze in the air, trembling but unable to come to rest. "I . . . I don't want to build anything without you." He gazed at her stern profile, willing her to turn, to look back at him. "Stay. With me."

She watched his hand hovering above hers. For a moment he thought she would take it.

Then her eyelashes fluttered, and her gaze fixed once more on the road, on the far horizon. "Your shade," she said. "It's ascendant now, isn't it?"

His brow tightened into a hard knot. He hesitated, then nodded.

"I can't perceive it." She cast a brief sideways glance. "No shadow senses." She shrugged, looking ahead once more. "But there is something different about you, something . . . something free." Her lips were very dry and chapped in the cold. When she bit them, they turned red and then went pale again almost at once. "I kept Laranta bound most of our life together. I restrained her, I . . . I tortured her. And she only offered love in return."

Her voice trailed off. The silence lasted so long, Terryn feared she would not speak again, feared she would simply spur her horse back into motion and be gone. But at last she turned and faced him. "I have nothing to give you, Terryn. I'm . . . empty."

"I don't care," he answered. "I'll love you enough for both of us."

She shook her head. Her dark eyes glistened, too bright. "I may know little of love, but I can tell you it doesn't work like that."

"All right." Terryn's hand clenched into a fist, leather reins twisted between his fingers. "All right then, don't stay. I'll go with you instead. I'll accompany you to the Skada Mountains, at least until I know you've found your home. I'll ask nothing of you. I'll be like a hunt brother. I'll simply be near to help you, and—"

"You're an idiot."

The words were sharp, but they sent a strange dart of joy to his heart. She sounded, just for a moment, like herself again. The joy shattered almost at once, however, when she continued, "You can't leave Gerard. We both know that. It would be like asking you to ride away without your right arm."

He opened his mouth. But what could he say? There was a soul tether binding him here as surely as Nisirdi was bound to him. He could not break it, no matter how he might wish to. "Ayleth," he began, uncertain where his words would take him, only knowing he couldn't give in, not yet. Not yet.

Before he could utter one word more, she dropped her reins, leaned suddenly in her saddle, and caught his face in both hands. Her fingers were like ice on his cheeks, and her lips were rough with cold as they found his mouth. But the jolt of heat that shot through him banished all other sensation. He reached for her, grabbed hold of her upper arms, gripping tight as though he could grasp her very spirit and compel her to stay with him.

She pulled back too soon, and though he tried to draw

her back to him again, she resisted. She didn't require shade strength to break his hold and put distance between them.

"When you've found what you're looking for," Terryn said, his voice a whisper in the frosty air, "will you return?"

She tilted her head to one side beneath the drape of her hood. "Don't wait for me, Terryn," she said. "Live your life. Serve your king. Think of me now and then. But don't wait for me."

With those words, she faced the road, leaned low over Chestibor's neck, and uttered a harsh, "*Yah!*" driving her heels into his ribs. The gelding surged into a gallop, eating up the distance and churning white snow like a blizzard behind him. Terryn watched from his saddle until that bright red hood vanished from sight.

CHAPTER 25

FEW SIGHTS WERE MORE BEAUTIFUL TO GERARD THAN the image of his wife seated across the room from him in one of the large study chairs pulled close to the fireplace. The way she sat with little Nilly in her lap, her head inclined over the child's shoulder, a book propped up in her lap . . . it was pure perfection.

The book was an illuminated manuscript full of strange colorful images and only a few elaborately wrought words. Cerine pointed out a gorgeously curlicued character, and Gerard heard her murmur, "N is for Nilly."

The child giggled. Gerard's heart swelled. It almost hurt to feel such joy. The world before him was full of shadows and uncertainty. In just three days, he would set forth from Dunloch with a large company and make his way to Telianor to lay claim to the crown of the Chosen King. He anticipated no great difficulty in this first stretch of his journey . . . the difficulties would come hard and fast thereafter, when he began the process of changing laws.

First and foremost, he must put laws in place to protect Nilly and children like her.

As for Nilly herself, he had already agreed to Cerine's proposal that they take her on as their legal ward. She would be raised under close supervision in Telianor, treated as a daughter in their house. They would do what they could to keep her inborn state concealed for as long as possible, but Gerard knew better than to expect the secret to last.

Still, he smiled. Those worries could wait for another day. Now was the time for admiring the fall of firelight on the gentle face of his wife, for admiring the curve of her cheek and the elegance of her long neck. For anticipating nightfall and their chance to slip away to their room together . . . and for remembering the night before and the too-short hours spent alone with each other in the dark.

His grin grew, and just at that moment Cerine looked up and met his eye. As though reading where his thoughts had led, she blushed and quickly looked down again, though he could see how her mouth twisted in her effort to hide a similar smile. But her voice continued in its steady, patient tones, praising Nilly as the little girl tried sounding out an experimental, "Nnnnnn."

A knock at the door interrupted Gerard's contemplation. Nilly and Cerine looked up from their book, their gazes turning to him, large eyed and a little anxious. Gerard gave them a reassuring nod before calling out, "Who's there?"

"It's me," Terryn's rough voice responded from the other side.

"Ah, yes, come in," Gerard said, and Terryn stepped into the room.

Nilly uttered a delighted squeal, a sound Gerard had never expected to hear from the small waif's mouth. She scrambled out of Cerine's lap and flung herself across the room into Terryn's arms. The tall venator knelt, accepting her embrace. His face was briefly hidden from Gerard's view behind her head as Nilly wrapped her arms around his neck. He stood, lifting her, and approached Gerard's desk with the child in his arms.

"We've had word from Bertheron Outpost in Nion. Venatrix Jeanne d'Eudes will be joining us on the road to Telianor."

"Excellent." Gerard nodded, satisfied. Kephan's network of connections among the farther castras in Gaulia were proving invaluable. Already five Evanderians had pledged their support to his new and heretical cause. The more Red Hoods he had riding with him to the capital, the better.

But he took a closer look at Terryn. Something wasn't right, something in his expression. The news he brought was good, but Terryn was strangely pale, his dark complexion gray on the edges and his eyes bright as though with fever. "Is something wrong?"

Terryn shook his head. Without a word he bowed—an awkward feat to accomplish with a child in his arms. Then he crossed the room to deposit Nilly back in Cerine's lap before offering a more elegant bow and a murmur of, "My queen," to Cerine. He left the room then without a glance Gerard's way.

Gerard watched him go, watched the door shut behind him, and frowned at its panels.

"Follow him."

Startled, he turned to see Cerine watching him closely from her chair. She nodded toward the door, her brows raised. "Go on," she urged.

He hesitated. Then, scraping his chair hard on the floor, he stood and dashed out from behind the desk and across the room. Opening the door, he spied Terryn at the end of the passage. "Terryn, wait," he called out.

Terryn turned and pulled himself to attention. He wouldn't quite meet his king's gaze as Gerard approached, looking off over his left shoulder instead.

Gerard regarded him closely. "Any news from Milisendis?"

"None, my king," Terryn replied crisply. "Kephan

believes Venatrix di Theldry will report to Dunloch on the morrow. She will certainly come before—"

"I mean Ayleth."

Terryn swallowed. If anything, he looked even paler than before. "Venatrix Ayleth will not be joining the royal entourage."

Gerard's heart stopped. "Do you mean she's . . ." He couldn't finish, uncertain what it was he feared.

But Terryn continued, his voice deceptively steady. "She has taken her leave of Wodechran Borough and returned to Drauval."

"What?" Gerard's brow puckered. "She left? Whatever for?"

"I believe her intention is to seek out the home of her childhood."

Gerard heard the words but didn't understand them. Hollis had given him a summary of Ayleth's history to the extent of her knowledge, and Terryn had filled him in on a few more details. But, if he was honest, most of it hadn't stuck. He'd been more than a little distracted these last three weeks. "Where . . . where is her childhood home?"

"Somewhere in the Skada Mountains."

"You mean to tell me Ayleth is riding alone into the Skada Mountains in the dead of winter. With no idea where she's going. And no shade power to draw from."

Terryn's gaze remained fixed on whatever it was that had arrested his attention beyond Gerard's shoulder. "Yes."

Gerard gaped at him. Then he huffed a sharp breath. "Then what in the Haunts-damn are you doing here, Terryn?"

Terryn blinked and finally looked directly at him. He didn't speak, but his eyes held a question.

"Why haven't you gone after her? Gone *with* her, for that matter?" Gerard flung up his hands and shook his head. "Don't think I don't know how you feel about her. I'm not blind. You love her, and you just let her ride off to certain death in the wilderness? What are you thinking, man?"

"I . . ." Terryn stopped, swallowed, and continued in a firmer voice. "You need me at your side, Gerard. Now more than ever, I must be with you. I am—"

"You're an idiot."

Terryn stopped again, then quietly said, "That seems to be the popular consensus."

"Go after her." Gerard reached out and grabbed Terryn's shoulder, squeezing hard. "Don't wait. Don't hesitate. Go after her, Terryn. Find her and help her and, if you can, bring her back. Or stay with her in the Goddess-forsaken wilderness if that's what the two of you prefer. But whatever you do, by the Three Holy Names, do *not* make me your excuse."

"Gerard . . ." Terryn's voice broke. He struggled, the lines around his mouth deepening as he mastered his voice. "What will you do? Without me to protect you, how can you—"

"I don't need you in my shadow, Terryn," Gerard said. "I can stand on my own two feet and face my own monsters, my own demons." He put his other hand up, gripping Terryn's shoulders and gazing into his eyes. "Go. Break this chain that has bound you to me all these years. And when you've found and won your love, come back if you can. But come only at your free will. Do you understand?"

Terryn's face broke. He caught Gerard and hauled him

close in an embrace that lasted only a moment but long enough.

Then he pulled away, turned, and rushed down the great staircase so fast, his cloak billowed out behind him. Gerard, standing at the gallery balustrade, watched him pass through the doors of Dunloch Keep and out into the fading daylight beyond. "Go in grace, brother," he whispered.

Back at his study door, just as he reached for the latch, peals of laughter met his ears—the voices of his wife and the inborn child, filled with mirth and joy. Gerard's soul lifted even as his heart ached. Silent tears fell from his eyes.

CHAPTER 26

Spring was breaking across the mountains when Ayleth finally rode into Gillanluòc Outpost. She dismounted Chestibor at the entrance. Her searching fingers swiftly found and pulled the secret mechanism, and the gate swung heavily open partway. Then stuck.

Muttering curses, Ayleth took hold of the wooden posts and pulled. She pulled again and again, finally getting it back into motion. By the time she had a space large enough for her horse to pass through, she was panting. Tasks that had once been so easy were much harder these days. She'd never realized how consistently she'd leaned on her shade powers, even when Laranta was under suppression.

But Laranta was gone. She was alone. She'd have to learn how to get by. At least for a little while longer.

Ayleth led Chestibor into the yard and across to the stable. It felt strangely cold and abandoned. Snow still mounded high up the walls. Part of the roof had caved in at one end, and with no venatrix home to shore it up and make repairs, the damage had only worsened. But Chestibor's old stall was still serviceable, and the rats hadn't gotten into the bin of oats. It took a brave rat indeed to stick its nose into a venatrix's stores.

After seeing to her horse's needs, Ayleth stepped back into the yard, facing the blockhouse. She stood for a moment, shoulders back, hands at her sides, breathing the chilly spring air. In and out. Slow and steady.

The pressure of memories surrounded her—memories of one solitary girl and her equally solitary mistress. Memories of target practice with her scorpiona, of dagger fights and hand-to-hand tussles. Her gaze pulled to the bonehouse, and a shudder rippled up her spine at the darker memories associated with that building. Death and blood and sorrow.

And everywhere, memories of Hollis.

They weren't false memories, were they? Certainly not all of them. They weren't lies. Her years spent as Hollis's apprentice, those years of devotion and service . . . there was truth there, waiting to be found.

But if those truths were built on a foundation of falsehood, what parts could she trust?

Ayleth crossed to the blockhouse and entered. It was as cold as a tomb, but she lit a fire on the hearth and threw open windows to admit the spring sunlight and air. The floor rushes smelled musty, but she wasn't planning to stay long, so she didn't bother grabbing a broom to sweep them out.

Despite what she'd told Terryn all those months ago, Ayleth had not set out for Drauval Borough right away. Although every instinct urged her to throw herself into this final hunt, she had accepted the truth: Without Laranta's magic and strength, she would not survive a winter in the mountains. Chestibor, at least, deserved better than death by freezing or starvation.

So, once she took the ferry across the river, Ayleth had set out for a town in Luquin Borough, far enough from Wodechran that she needn't fear discovery should anyone be foolish enough to pursue her. Her skill sets were limited, but she didn't need a venatrix's poisons or a shade's supernatural senses to bring down natural prey, so she'd managed to convince a local bailiff to give her and her horse shelter in exchange for her hunting skills. Throughout the winter she kept the town supplied with rabbits, pheasants, and even deer. She charged little for her service—room and board for her horse and herself—and the townsfolk enjoyed fresh meat throughout the winter instead of the usual smoked or dried fare.

During that time, she kept her red hood tucked away out of sight. Folks tended to stare at her stubbly scalp and her ugly scars, but no one asked questions. She kept to herself, she did her job, and so the winter passed. At the first signs of spring, Ayleth had taken her leave, packed up Chestibor, and set her course for the northern mountains.

Hollis had left a stash of fuel in the box. Ayleth

brought in more logs, adding them to the fire, which now crackled bright on the hearth. As the low-ceilinged room began to warm, she looked around at Hollis's desk and the alcoves built into the wall alongside the stone chimney.

Much though she wanted to simply set out for the higher, wilder ranges of Skada, she knew that would be foolish. She would never find what she was looking for unless she had a goal of some sort in mind. The mountains were too sprawling, the forests too deep. And her mortal senses were too limited.

A few months ago, she wouldn't necessarily have minded leaving her horse behind and wandering off into the wilderness to face whatever adventure she found before finally succumbing to foe or fate. But over the winter, during the cold months of checking snares and sighting deer along the scope of her scorpiona, she'd had time. Time to realize that she didn't want to simply throw her life away in a suicide journey.

She wanted to find answers. If any answers remained to be found.

So, as the fire crackled and her numb limbs slowly

loosened with warmth, Ayleth set to work going through Hollis's books and papers. She found the small skin-bound volume containing the list of the Crimson Devils and took a moment to scratch out those last seven names on the final page. The action gave her less satisfaction than she'd hoped. But at least the list was now complete.

An hour into her search, she pulled out Hollis's copy of Saint Evander's holy writ and paged carefully through it on the chance her former mistress may have hidden something inside. She came, inevitably, to a page much yellowed on the edges from all the times it had been turned to over the years. She didn't need to read it. Her lips naturally moved, quoting each line word for word:

A poison will spread through the heart of my people, giving rise to Falsehood reigning in the name of Truth. But I will send a champion. I will send the man whom I have chosen to cut off the poison's head and lead the people back to Me. Brother with brother, one shade-taken and one untaken, will stand together, establishing a new kingdom under My Name.

Thus will the Golden Age be brought to pass.

Ayleth's mouth hardened into a grim line. Over the last few months, she had learned to block out remembrance of that terrible night. But now her hand crept to her brow, feeling the scar wrapped around her head and across her brow. Images flash behind her eyes. And that feeling. That indescribable feeling of absolute power that had been hers for those brief and eternal moments.

But it was Gerard's arm that swung the sword. Gerard's arm that cut off the Witch Queen's head. True, he was only acting as Ayleth's puppet, and thus the *Cravan Druch* was broken, the curse of blood fulfilled. But it was Gerard who held the blade.

Was it possible that the *Seion-Ebathe* was fulfilled despite everything? Despite all the mistakes, all the lies, all the manipulations of men . . . had the Chosen King come to Perrinion after all?

Ayleth closed the book and set it aside. She shouldn't let herself think about these things. She shouldn't let herself wonder if Gerard and his entourage had arrived in Telianor. She shouldn't allow herself to muse on the doings at court, on the changes that must even now be rippling across the kingdom. She shouldn't allow herself to wish that she were there, standing at the king's back, standing at Terryn's side . . .

None of that was her concern anymore.

Ayleth turned away from the book and the table, away from the fire and the warmed front room of the blockhouse. She climbed the rickety stair up to the second story and entered Hollis's bedroom, where she threw open chests, dug under the mattress, and pulled up floorboards, searching with abandon. Now and then she felt a pang of remorse for invading her mistress's privacy, but these pangs she quickly silenced. Hollis had invaded her mind. As far as Ayleth was concerned, Hollis had lost her right to privacy.

At last, she found a little partition hidden in the wall, and when her questing fingers reached into the spider-webbed darkness, they touched something. Grasping its edge, she pulled out a little leather-bound volume. A logbook.

Her breath suddenly unsteady, she pulled it free and undid the leather straps holding the soft covers shut. Sitting on Hollis's bed, she laid the book open and checked the date on the first page—fourteen years ago.

This was it. This must be the one.

She began to flip through the pages, scanning Hollis's familiar penmanship, reading of hunts and interviews and official notes to be sent in reports to the castra. Here and there she discovered scraps of notes that caught her attention—rumors Hollis had picked up across the borough about a black wolf and her sentient, shade-taken pack. Rumors of a wild child running with beasts. Rumors which Hollis collected with greater fervor and frequency as the log progressed.

At last Ayleth came to the note she was looking for. A location: Rasse Valley.

Her mouth turned up at one corner. Now, she just needed a map.

Two weeks later, Ayleth walked in the flesh through memories of her childhood.

It was strange to her how familiar this forest was—this forest she had walked so many times in her mindscape without realizing that it was all a memory. These pine-covered slopes, these crests, these gorges, this flowing river. She had covered this ground time and again in her thoughts.

Four days ago she had left Chestibor behind, paying a farmer for his keep with a small store of coins she'd found at Gillanluòc and promising to return for him soon. She hadn't wanted to risk her beloved horse in such rough country, preferring to make the venture on foot.

The deeper she traveled into Rasse Valley, the lighter her steps became, the more freely she moved. Her body assumed a different gait and stance, as though simply by breathing the air of this valley and walking beneath these trees, she would revert to patterns of her childhood. She had to consciously resist the odd temptation to shed layers of clothing. But she wasn't a child anymore; she no longer had Laranta's strength and senses coursing through her body. She was tall and strong, but she was limited by her own mortality.

She hunted game to feed herself, set up camp at night, and cooked whatever she caught and killed and dressed. She slept wrapped in her cloak and blankets, for the nights were still bitter.

And always, always she listened for a chorus of wolves

in the darkness. But she never heard them.

At last, on the fourth day of wandering, her feet found a slope more familiar than the rest. It seemed almost as though she could . . . *smell* the long-ago presence of her brothers and sisters. Their names came to her lips again as she climbed: "Dulrudu, Rotoro, Rhadarka, Ilrili, and Nenete . . ."

Far up the slope, in a clear space where only three trees managed to hold tenaciously to the harsh soil and rock, she found a den. It was smaller than she remembered. She crouched at its mouth, peering into the shadows within. The smells were there still, so old and so distant that her mortal senses almost missed them.

She remembered lying inside that shelter as thunder rolled over the mountain. She remembered a tangle of furry limbs and tails, of hot breath and glinting eyes. She remembered strange voices speaking into her head in a language unlike mortal tongue. A language without words. She had all but forgotten.

She turned away, sitting at the mouth of the den, and gazed out across the valley spread below. The sun was beginning to sink in the western sky, and soon she would need to find a place to make camp for the night. For now, she simply sat and stared, her mind empty, her heart still.

Then she bowed her head, and the tears came in a torrent.

"Why?" she whispered. She tasted salt in her mouth, filling her tongue with its sting. "Why, Laranta? Why did you leave me? Why?"

There was no answer. How could there be? Laranta was gone, gone, gone. Lost to the Haunts. Suffering her eternal torment. While Ayleth was here, whole in body, empty in spirit. Her heart too warped with pain to be of any use to her, to anyone.

"I said we'd never be parted," she whispered. Then she threw back her head and shouted at the sky, let her voice ring against the stones and fall to the valley below. "Why didn't you take me with you? Why did you leave me behind?"

Her voice bounced, echoed, rolled away. Somewhere off to her left, a bird took flight, startled out of its roost by the sudden clamor. Then all was still again.

Ayleth bent her head. Her jaw ached as she clenched it tight. Then sobs broke through her bared teeth, and tears dampened the stones at her feet. She had not wept since the first night of her loss. These tears were different. Those had been tears of frantic denial, hot and wrathful. These . . . these were bitter tears. Painful, every one of them, as they glided down her cheeks. Tears of despair.

Mistress.

A growl in the air, distant as a storm.

A memory. Just a memory. One of the many clamoring in her head, here in this place of memories.

Mistress.

Shaking her head, Ayleth pushed the hood back over her shoulders and grasped at the short hair of her scalp, pulling as though she could rip that voice right out of her mind. But it remained. Soft, distant. Insistent.

Mistress.

"*Laranta.*" She looked up. And there was a shadow before her in the fading sunlight. A shadow that wasn't shadow. It couldn't be Laranta, because Laranta was always darkness personified, but this was . . . not darkness. Not shadow. Not light either. Brilliant and invisible and present.

Ayleth reached out her hands. A face hovered just in

front of hers, nose to nose. A face so painfully familiar and yet entirely unknown. Her mortal senses perceived nothing, yet . . . somehow, she thought she felt soft fur beneath her fingers. She gazed into eyes that were fierce and terrible and beautiful and full of love. And beyond those eyes, beyond the formless image was a near-blinding aura. A song. A greatness Ayleth couldn't bear to see. She had to look away from it or risk everything.

So she gazed into that unshadowed face before her.

Mistress.

I love.

Ayleth blinked—

And she was sitting on the stones outside the mouth of an empty wolf's den. The sun had set, and the stars spread above her in innumerable bounty. A crescent moon glided through their ranks like a small boat on a vast black ocean.

Ayleth shook her head, stood up, and looked around. How long had she been sitting here? Had she fallen asleep? Had she dreamed?

She looked down at her hand, which was clenched so tightly that her nails dug into her skin. With an effort she forced her fingers to uncurl. There in her palm lay strands of shining fur that glittered in the starlight and then dissipated to nothing.

She must be tired. Or hungry. Or sick. She must be losing her mind with grief and solitude. Or perhaps . . .

Movement caught her eye.

Instinct jolted through Ayleth's veins, and she turned, sinking into a defensive crouch, her hand reaching for her knife. Something appeared down below, slipping through a stand of trees and stepping from the shadows into the dim light. The shape was long, low, lean. A wolf.

Ayleth's heart thudded hard but not with fear. She rose slowly from her crouch, her hand still resting on the hilt of her knife, but her fingers relaxed. She waited.

The wolf took a few more steps into the open, then stopped. Its head came up, its ears pricked forward.

Is that you?

The voice appeared in her head. A voice she knew, ringing in a wordless language of song, a low growling cadence.

She gasped and took a step forward. "Rotoro?"

The wolf tilted its head. Then it whined softly.

Ayleth sprang into action, scrambling over stones and down the slope, quickly covering the distance between her and the beast. "Rotoro!" she cried again. The memories were vivid in her head—her wolf sister, the only one of the pack who bore a black coat like their mother's. The wolf lifted her head higher. Moonlight revealed that her face was no longer black but mostly white, and age clouded her golden eyes. She flashed her teeth, growling, but not with anger.

Ayleth didn't hesitate to drop to her knees before the huge old animal. She didn't hesitate to throw her arms around that shaggy black neck. And it was so familiar—it was something she'd done a thousand times with Laranta, but always in her mind. Long years had passed since she'd embraced a physical being like this.

Sister, sang the voice in her head. *My little mortal sister. Where is my other sister? Where is Laranta? I heard her voice up here in the heights, and I came hunting for her, for you. Is she not with you?*

Ayleth shook her head, her face still buried in that ruff of fur. It smelled like pine and blood and wolf. It smelled like home. "Laranta is gone," she said.

Speak to me in our language, sister, Rotoro said. *Or do you not remember how?*

"It's been so long," Ayleth whispered. She pulled back and looked into Rotoro's face, looked beyond the wolf, beyond the cloudy eyes to the shade spirit that dwelled inside. "I'm sorry, Rotoro," Ayleth said. "I'm sorry I left you. I'm sorry I was gone for so long."

So long? Rotoro tilted her old head. Her body sagged suddenly and sank to the ground, its ribcage expanding and retracting with the labor of her breaths. *What is time, little sister, to spirits like ours?*

Ayleth frowned, passing her hand over Rotoro's head, down her neck, and over her side. "Time might not matter to the spirit," she said, "but our bodies are a different matter. What is wrong with your body, Rotoro?"

It is fading, the wolf shade answered. *I have held on for years now, years beyond the natural span of this host. I have held on in hopes that you would return. Now that these eyes have seen you, they will see no more. I must let this host pass.*

"But what of *you?*" Ayleth's heart began to ache again, a too familiar sensation. She stroked the wolf's head, her hand shaking hard. "I've . . . I've only just found you. Will

I lose you already? Like all the others?"

I hope not, little sister. I hope not.

With those words, the wolf laid its head down on the rock and closed its eyes. Its ribcage expanded again with one last, laborious intake of air. Then, as it let out that breath in a stream of white, its life went out, and its spirit poured free into the ether.

"Rotoro!" Ayleth cried. Then, in her heart, she cried out louder still in a language not of the mortal world. *"Rotoro! Don't go! Come back to me, come dwell inside me. There is room for you with me. Come, sister, please!"*

There was brightness. There was pain—a stabbing pain to her eye, brief and yet excruciating. Ayleth screamed, falling backwards, and lay still as death, staring up at the stars overhead. They spun slowly in their dancelike patterns, distant and unconcerned with the doings of the world so far below.

Ayleth closed her eyes. She stepped into the pine forest of her mind and stood there in the quiet shadows with long dark hair flowing down her bare back. *"Rotoro?"* she called, her voice echoing against the trunks. *"Rotoro, are you here?"*

I am here, sister.

A shape coalesced before her, shadowy formlessness pulling together into the image of a wolf. Not Laranta. Laranta was gone, and the ache of her loss would remain with Ayleth forever. But she gazed at this new spirit, at this sister she had thought lost forever.

She smiled.

EPILOGUE

AT DAWN THE NEXT DAY, AYLETH RAN THROUGH THE mountains, through the trees, feeling the power of a Feral shade course through her body. Beside her loped the insubstantial yet altogether real image of a black wolf, its mouth open in an animal smile, its tongue lolling, its ears pricked as though for the hunt. They raced together along the banks of the river, then turned into the trees and climbed a steep slope, higher and higher, until they broke out from the forest and achieved the clear air above.

Ayleth stood on a boulder with Rotoro at her side. She breathed deep of the mountain and the forest and the wildness all around her, and her heart was light, lighter than she'd believed it ever could be again. Her mortal body panted with exertion, and her blood pounded in her temples. Sweat ran in rivulets through her short hair. She wiped droplets off her brow before they could drip into her eyes. Then she blinked, shifting from mortal vision to shadow sight.

"*Rotoro,*" she said. "*What do you see in the distance there?*"

The wolf shade tilted her head, eyes keen and searching as she gazed out across the valley. *A shade,* she said. *A mighty shade indeed. One I have not seen before. Do you know it, little sister?*

Ayleth nodded slowly. She gazed across the forests to the far side of the valley, admiring the sweep of a great light-dragon's wings, the elegant way it rose in the air, arched, and dove once more. A shimmering soul tether ran down into the trees below.

She knew to whom that tether was attached. She knew to whom this shade belonged.

So, he'd come after her, searching for her through the

winter and the spring. Perhaps he'd found his way to Gillanluòc, perhaps he'd found the logbook, which she'd left behind on the table in the front room, open to the page on which *Rasse Valley* was written. Or perhaps he was simply following the instincts of his heart.

"*Yes,*" Ayleth said. "*I know who that is.*" She looked down at Rotoro, and her heart glowed with warmth. "*I have someone I need to introduce to you. And then . . .*"

She smiled softly and spoke aloud in her mortal voice. "And then, it's time for us to go home."

ABOUT THE AUTHOR

Sylvia Mercedes makes her home in the idyllic North Carolina countryside with her handsome husband, sweet baby-lady, and Gummy Bear, the Toothless Wonder Cat. When she's not writing she's . . . okay, let's be honest. When she's not writing, she's running around after her little girl, cleaning up glitter, trying to plan healthy-ish meals, and wondering where she left her phone. In between, she reads a steady diet of fantasy novels. But mostly she's writing.

After a short career in Traditional Publishing (under a different name), Sylvia decided to take the plunge into the Indie Publishing World and is enjoying every minute of it. The Venatrix Chronicles is her first series as an independent author, but she's got many more planned!

Don't miss the thrilling new series by Sylvia Mercedes!

A clever thief.
A disgraced mage.
A kiss of poison . . . .

THE SCARRED MAGE OF ROSEWARD

Meanwhile be sure to read Song of Shadows:

Visit www.SylviaMercedesBooks.com
to get your free copy.

www.ingramcontent.com/pod-product-compliance
Lightning Source LLC
Chambersburg PA
CBHW030244060726
47498CB00002BA/254